ISOLATION JUNCTION

Flying free from emotional abuse

Jennifer Gilmour

Copyright © 2018 Jennifer Gilmour
Second Edition
Published by Pict Publishing

ISBN: 978 1 9999647 1 9

The checklist Rose takes in Chapter Ten has been sourced from the Women's Aid website (www.womensaid.org.uk).

A CIP catalogue record for this book is available from the British Library.

Cover copyright © Pict Publishing/Jennifer Gilmour
Cover image copyright © Bigstock/PathDoc/Tawng

Pict Publishing
Empowered Voices

Acknowledgements

Thank you firstly to Leanne Marshall at Pict Publishing. I joined Pict Publishing knowing that I would be supported by the amazing women who are under the umbrella of Pict. You have listened to what my own vision was for this book and have made it blossom with the creation of the cover and support with queries I have had since I joined. I am truly honoured to be a part of such empowering voices.

Thank you to Emma Mitchell from Creating Perfection who gave artistic direction in the republication of this novel. Thank you for having many conversations with me about the emotions, voice and message of this book. I am more than delighted to have you as my editor knowing that I am secure in your hands with the sensitive aspects of my work. I consider you a friend and know that you will be a part of my journey ahead.

To my fellow authors who have taken their time out of their busy schedules to help, guide and support me; I thank you.

To the selfless work of bloggers who take time out to help promote not only my work but many writers in the world, you are incredibly valuable and without you I would have felt partially alone in the world of blogging. I continue to learn from you, be inspired by you, be encouraged and motivated to continue what I do.

Thank you

Thank you to those who supported by pledging in the original Kickstarter campaign for the first edition, which took place July and August 2016. Without your support, the vision would have been restricted and you were the first to stand with me and begin to block the road to Isolation Junction. Thank you to the following people who pledged their support:

Amanda McCormick
Beat Mueller
Becka Simm
Beckie Brothers
Biddie Atkinson
Burt Jarratt
Claire Capper
Dawn Melbourne
Debbie Mawer
Denise Allen
Dianne Woodford
Gill Botterill
Hannah Maiden
Heather Benstead
Irene Furber
Jackie Woolnough
Jan McKinley
Jenna Jones
Jo Howarth
Joanne Jamieson
John Redhead
Jude Lennon
Judith Gilmour
Julie Aldcroft
Justyna Cieslinska
Linda Harper

Linda Mulholland
Lisa Preston
Lisa Southall
Mary Osborne
Michala Leyland
(Wood for The Trees Coaching)
Michele Stevenson
Michelle Emma Ogborne
Michelle Peters
Nicci Simmonds
Nicky Bartley
Paul Harper
Robin Gilmour
Sandra Bingley
Sarah Brock
Sharon Bosker
Sharon Kearns
Stacey Gales
Stephanie Hemsted
Sue Blaylock
Suze Dunkling
(Ellie Harvey Silver)
Suzie Oulton
Tammy Middleton
Vicki Sparks

This book is dedicated to the thousands of people who find themselves, through no fault of their own, in relationships ruled by domestic abuse and to my wonderful husband, children, family and friends who gave me the courage and the means to break free and to live my life free of control.

You know who you are and I love you all.

Introduction

As a passionate advocate for women in abusive relationships, I have amalgamated and fictionalised other survivors' experiences and research alongside my own experience to write my first novel.

This details the journey of a young woman from the despair of an emotionally abusive and unhappy marriage to happiness by having the confidence to challenge and change her life and to love again.

I hope that in reading my book, I will raise awareness of this often hidden and unseen behaviour and empower women in abusive relationships to seek help for themselves and to find the confidence to change their lives for the better.

The challenge is to bring about more widespread awareness of emotional abuse and coercive behaviour. My goal is for these aspects of controlling behaviour to be talked about more openly, to reach MPs and the national news for their support and to further change perceptions and policies so that people in these emotionally charged situations have a voice.

These changes are necessary to help and protect women not just from former partners but also from some of the inappropriate and inadequate decisions made within the family and magistrates' courts which, often unwittingly, leave women isolated and trapped. I appeal to all of you reading this to help 'Block the Road to Isolation Junction'.

CHAPTER ONE

Ice-cold rain splattered her face; her toes and fingers were numb and yet she sat there huddled up and gently rocking herself. It was a black night with no stars, like someone had just switched off the sky. The only light shining on her face was the orange glow from a single street light.

Rose couldn't cope anymore, she was crying into her hands so hard it hurt her heart; a deep spike of a pain rushing through her body and not for the first time. She had felt this pain for what felt an eternity and it sometimes shocked her when she realised it had been five years.

She sat in the mud in front of a run-down, old church, surrounded by old and wonky gravestones, soaked to the bone but she didn't care, she'd learnt to detach herself from her feelings and thoughts. She was like a robot.

Rose's mind was racing through those years in which she suffered and wasted with Darren. Better known as Den – a name she'd always hated – he was a short and overweight man in his thirties and tonight he'd finished with her, again, but this time, Rose wasn't going to go back. It was a regular occurrence from Den to try to keep her in his possession by panicking her. He didn't realise that this time, Rose was going to stand up to him, she just didn't know how right now.

Her parents had never approved of Darren, mainly because of the ten-year age gap.

'You're young and naïve,' they'd said to her after the first introduction.

'He's not the type of man you normally go for either,' Rose's mum had said, and she was right. Rose did have a type and Darren wasn't it.

'He treats me like a princess, and no one has ever complimented me like he does,' Rose had explained to her parents, thinking it was good to deviate from her usual type.

She was naturally pretty and her thick, long, red hair was the envy of many of her friends when they were growing up. Darren adored her curvy figure and made her feel like no one had before. She thought her parents were being ageist and that they'd eventually come around.

They were right, of course, and now she wondered why she hadn't listened to them. Why hadn't she taken the countless offers of escape when she became trapped?

Thinking back, the signs were there but who would have known, or believed, everything that had happened would lead to where she was?

Rose closed her eyes and thought back over the events that had led to her being sat wet and alone in the dark and in the most impossible situation she could have imagined.

* * *

Rose was getting ready for a night out with her new boyfriend, Darren. The plan was for her girlfriends and Darren's mates to all get together.

Lyndsey was blonde, ditzy, and always seemed to end up with her heart broken. Helen was a brunette and constantly had a smile on her face. Rose couldn't wait to get everyone together as they hadn't seen each other as a group for ages and they all loved going out on the town.

She'd spent an hour curling her hair, she thought she'd probably put too much make-up on. The music was loud, the drinks were flowing, and she was bopping along to the music while singing into her hairbrush.

The house had a musky smell, a mixture of smoke, perfume, aftershave, whiskey, and burning hair.

Once ready, Rose felt high with confidence – it wasn't often she felt this pretty. The six-inch stiletto heels enhanced her legs and gave the illusion they never ended; the short, red dress flared out slightly at the ends, had a high waistline, and showed off hour-glass figure to perfection.

After taking a selfie for Instagram, Rose turned to Darren expecting him to do his usual skit of pretending to be knocked off his seat while telling her he was, *blown away by her beauty*.

But this time was different, he barely acknowledged her, never mind gave her a compliment. Walking towards him as sexily as possible to get a reaction, Rose tried to sit on his lap when she reached him, Den stopped her from sitting on his lap with one look that made her think she'd done something wrong. It seemed very much out of character for him and after a couple of drinks, Rose was feeling playful.

Was he playing hard to get? she thought.

Darren clearly wasn't interested in Rose's efforts, he had his cigar at the side of his mouth, whiskey glass in one hand, phone in the other, and he barely took his eyes off the screen.

Feeling dejected, Rose sat next to him and checked her own phone to see where Lyndsey and Helen were. Half hour had passed, and Darren hadn't once acknowledged her once.

'Den, everyone's just getting into their taxi, are we ready?' Rose nudged him to encourage him to make a move.

Darren seemed to shake himself together and said, 'Yep... sorry... I was in my own world there.'

Rose was baffled a bit but still asked him, 'So, what do you think?' and she got up and gave him a twirl and blew him a kiss.

'Yeah, you look great.'

His comment seemed forced to her, usually his jaw hit the floor, and he'd want to take photos. She tried again and gave him a huge smile and went to kiss his lips, but he started giggling and soon erupted into laughter. Glancing in the mirror, Rose thought she must have had a make-up smudge, or her hair was out of place, but she was immaculate.

'What's funny, Den?' Rose asked feeling she'd missed something.

Now almost crying with laughter Den looked up at Rose and remarked, 'I never realised just how big your smile was.'

Confusion fogged her mind, and she didn't know whether it was a compliment or not. He eventually stood up and put his hand on her cheek.

'You have a beautiful smile, it's huge.' There was an awkward pause, before he continued, 'But it's so big; I hadn't noticed before; you have a Joker smile – you know, like Heath Ledger in the *Dark Knight*. He cut the sides of his mouth, so he was always smiling!' And he laughed again. 'Sorry, I can't look at you right now, that's all I see.'

Rose was confused, hurt, and upset, why would he say something like this? Rose told herself not to get too upset about it but called him a twat in her head. Rose didn't quite know how to respond.

'I'm just going to the bathroom before we go.' There was a slight shake in her voice, a dry throat had developed, and she found it hard to swallow.

She took a small glass out of the mirrored cabinet above the sink, filled it will cold water, and took a sip, then shut the cabinet door and stared at herself. Feeling anxious she took a deep breath and fanned her face with her hands, she raised her lips.

What am I afraid of? I need to look for myself. Is it really that funny? Her pearly white teeth came out and she couldn't see what the problem was, she saw a part of her she liked, a feature that others had complimented her on.

In that moment, Rose felt something wasn't right; there's taking the mick out of someone and then there's laughing *at* someone. Den's reaction didn't sit right with her and she became self-conscious of the beautiful smile she was once happy to wear across her face.

Rose had managed to put it all aside by the time they got to the pub, alcohol was good at taking her hurt away. Lyndsey and Helen were very welcoming and happy to spend time with her, they spent a lot of time dancing and having shot after shot. With each shot Rose loosened up and was able to enjoy the night, Den didn't mention her smile again; it was as though he was pretending nothing had happened.

Later in the night, the group were on their way home, the girls were gossiping, and the boys were walking with each other. Everyone was drunk and were having to shout at each other as their ears were still buzzing from the music in the nightclub. They arrived at their favourite takeaway, La Piazza, where the staff knew them all by name, at around 4.00 a.m. Darren was with his mates and Rose kept catching each his eye, they were blowing kisses and winking at each other with giggles. A couple who loved to flirt with each other, or what it looked like to everyone else.

Rose was the last in the queue when the security guard asked her to move to the other side of the counter as she was leaning on the glass cabinet like it was her pillow. Summoning up the energy and with the security guard's assistance she started to move when Darren came barging over, ready to start a fight with him. The bouncer was tall, muscular, and not someone you would mess with.

Rose was in a daze and didn't really know what was going on until she was pulled outside without the cheesy chips she was pining for. Lindsey was keeping Rose upright with her arm over her shoulder as they watched the security guard thumping Darren in the gut and winding him. Darren's friends picked him up and told him to walk on and apologised for his actions.

Still oblivious to what had happened inside, Rose asked Darren, 'What on Earth is going on?' A hiccup forcing its way out halfway through her question.

Mike, one of Darren's best friends, had sobered up with the drama. 'I don't really know, I just know it was something to do with you and that security guard.'

Rose was baffled and went over to ask Darren if he was OK; he was coughing, and Rose put her arm round him to comfort him – he shrugged her off hard and gave her a look that said, *I will never forget.*

'Come on, Rose, why don't you go home with the girls? Let him cool down?' Mike said, but she refused.

'If you can help me get him home, we'll be fine, honestly,' she replied.

The group set off on their journey home, it wasn't too far, and it was a calm night with only a slight breeze in the air. Darren didn't speak to or look at Rose the whole way there.

As planned, Mike left Darren and Rose at the top of the street, he continued to walk Lyndsey and Helen home. Darren had sobered up and didn't want any of Rose's assistance the last of the way home. Staying silent, she didn't know what to say or how to break the ice, she felt like the dizziness was relieved from the walk and fresh air, but she still felt queasy. Taking the house key out of her bag, Rose unlocked the door and made her way inside; Darren shoved his way past her.

Rose daren't speak a word and just shut the door.

'I can't believe you!' he screamed like Rose had done something horrendously wrong and had kept his frustration bottled up until they were alone.

'Why... what?'

Darren, shocked that Rose didn't know what was wrong, the confused look on his face soon flushed with irritation. He went through his pockets, got out a cigar, lit it up, took a drag, and visibly relaxed as he inhaled.

Rose removed a bobble from her wrist and put her hair up into a messy bun, it was starting to annoy her, and she felt less clammy once it was up. She didn't know what to do or say while she waited for him to calm down but thought she'd try.

'Well, I had a good night. It was funny when Lyndsey and Mike were on the pole wasn't it?' she said and laughed nervously.

Darren didn't laugh. In fact, he was getting angry and raised his voice louder. 'So, when that security guard came up to you, you thought you would let him get away with it?'

Rose wasn't sure what he was talking about and her face showed it.

'Come on... you know what I'm talking about, you liked it.'

Rose remained clueless and Darren took a long drag of

his cigar and walked towards her, stopped in front of her and blew all the smoke to the side so it went past her face. Rose just stood there, he looked her right in the eye.

'You will never look at another man like that ever again! You are *my* girlfriend and only I can look at you like that.' He was getting uncomfortably close to Rose – his nose was nearly touching hers. 'Do you understand?' Rose nodded in response, her heart started to race faster.

'Well, come on... *Do you understand?*' He growled in her face, she could feel the moisture from his breath.

With no hesitation Rose replied, 'Yes.' She felt she couldn't say no. But, that wasn't good enough for Den, he didn't trust her.

'I don't believe you!' Rose felt a hot and sharp pain on the back of her shoulder. As she scratched it Darren took his cigar off her and said, 'You're mine.' And he walked away. The pain was starting to come to the surface and she could smell her skin burning.

Gritting her teeth and sounding like a snake hissing, Rose was left in the room on her own, she tried to keep calm, but it was really starting to hurt, and her nausea was increasing. With Darren out of sight, Rose ran to the kitchen sink and vomited, before she grabbed some kitchen roll and tried to get her shoulder under the cold tap.

It proved difficult and meant she was having to bend in a way that she shouldn't be able to bend, but she needed to feel some relief from the burning. She spent the next hour under the tap trying to soothe the pain and she sobbed. She still had no idea why he'd do this to her, even if something had happened, she didn't deserve to be scarred for life like this.

* * *

There were times they did enjoy being together, but it never lasted long.

One night they were playing games on the PlayStation 3; crisps, pizzas, and chocolates were scattered all around them as they played. They were playing Bubble Pop and for a change, Rose was winning. They'd been laughing and joking for a couple of hours but after another win, Darren's mood soon changed. The atmosphere went from fun and flirty to suffocating and intense within seconds and Rose knew she needed to get out of there.

Faking a yawn, she said, 'Well, that's me done, babe. I'm going to nip to the loo then head to bed.'

The look Darren gave her made her sit back down. No second thought. No argument. Rose knew now what those looks meant. She picked her controller back up and waited for the next round to start.

'You will play this fucking game until I beat you and don't even think about letting me win, I *will* know,' he growled at her, eyes fixated on the television screen as he pressed start.

Rose continued winning, and it appeared Den had given up and she knew he'd use it as an excuse to start another argument with her. The frustration built until he couldn't take it anymore.

He jumped up from the sofa and pulled the console off the shelf, his controller and the wires along with it. Rose remained on the sofa fixed in position, knowing it was best not to respond as he roared and threw the computer across the room and watched as it smashed into a mirror.

'That was my aunt's mirror!' Rose cried. 'Why would you do that? You know how much it means to me.'

Rose was devastated. Her aunt had died the year before and Rose had been by her side every step of the way. They'd had an unbreakable bond, Rose would often describe her as her grandma, mum, sister, and best friend all wrapped into one. Aunt July was the most special person in her life.

Tears rolled down Rose's face as she stared at the broken pieces of the mirror. Her aunt had given her a love like none before, the type that made you feel secure, confident, and special and seeing the shattered glass made her pine for her aunt's favourite perfume to tickle her nostrils, but most of all, the arms of the most wonderful person to be around her.

Why didn't I just keep calm and play the game? Why is he so competitive? It's all my fault, why can't I learn not to react? I shouldn't have been good at something as petty as this and I shouldn't have enjoyed it, in fact I shouldn't have taken his control away from him. I should have behaved myself.

How could he do this to me? Does he like seeing me hurt? He knew what that mirror meant to me? Nothing can replace it and I don't think I can forgive him for this. I can't hold back the tears or hurt, can I? Darren doesn't seem to be bothered, will he even admit to doing something wrong? Will he even attempt to apologise?

CHAPTER TWO

A few months passed, and things seemed to settle down, Rose was beginning to preempt the arguments or the triggers that would set Den off. She hadn't spent much time with Helen and Lyndsey since the night out, but tonight they were going back to what used to be their weekly date night.

Together they laughed and giggled, had some stupidly drunk nights out, and shared a lot of secrets.

They had been to see a film, a romantic comedy; their default choice. They had an inability to be able to deal with sad films and horror films were banned completely as Lyndsey would scream, scare the audience, and get them thrown out. Laughter would often overtake them, and they would look like three giddy teenage girls.

Rose had planned to meet Darren after the film, so he could walk her home but didn't turn up; instead, he'd sent Rose a text message saying, *gone home* – which seemed odd to her especially as there were no kisses to end the message.

Lyndsey offered her a lift home, which she accepted, and more giggles were had for a few more minutes.

Rose eventually stepped into the terraced house she

shared with Darren; it was a small, two-bedroom property with the bathroom on the ground floor. Rose called it cosy despite it feeling claustrophobic at times, and she'd it was perfect because it was in walking distance of everywhere they needed to be.

They had moved in together when Darren's two housemates had moved abroad, and Rose's tenancy agreement had come to an end. It seemed like the perfect solution to their housing problems at the time.

Quieting her laughter and taking a deep breath, Rose made her way through the hall like she was going to be in trouble with her parents; a teenager coming back home after a night out on the town. As she passed the living room, she noticed the dim retro filament lamp was on in the far corner she went in to turn it off before realising Darren was in the room. It was like there was a spotlight shining above her head and down to the floor and outside this circle of light the rest of the room was dark and hard to see; Rose felt as if she was about to be interrogated, the air was cool, but the palms of her hands and the back of her neck were sweating.

Darren was sat in the armchair in the corner, slowly taking drags from his cigarette, he looked over at Rose like she was something stuck to the bottom of his shoe. Rose told him how much fun she'd had and wondered where he'd got to.

'I was looking forwards to ending the evening with you.' Rose said and cleared her throat, feeling anxious. Darren just sniggered, and it became obvious he wasn't happy.

'Seems like you've had a lot of fun without me.' He didn't blink, his eyes fixated on her. Rose was lost for words and couldn't read where this conversation was going or why he was glaring at her so coldly.

'I... erm, well, I always have fun with Lyndsey and

Helen, it was good to catch up with them, but, of course, it's good to see you now,' she said giving him with a cheeky smile, the one he knew to be *that* special signal. Rose hoped this would cut the ice as, for some reason, her nerves were starting to tingle. Darren didn't look impressed at all and Rose's nerves started to show in her voice as she spoke again, 'Anyway, I'm tired so I'm going to get to bed.'

It was a cold night and winter was almost upon them, so she quickly got into her PJs and after snuggling up in the duvet, it didn't take long for her to warm up. Putting Darren's behaviour to the back of her mind she had visions of Lyndsey and Helen making her laugh as she replayed the evening, then closing her eyes, she turned over, and fell asleep.

What felt like seconds later, Darren was straddling her, shaking her, and screaming in her face, 'Rose, Rose, we have to sort this out!'

At first, Rose thought there was an emergency and her heart was racing from the adrenaline. 'What do we need to sort out? What's happened?'

Disorientated and panicky, she rubbed her eyes and sat up.

'Well, the fact that you think you can go out whenever you want and be with whoever you want,' Darren said, implying that she'd had an affair.

'I don't know what you're talking about, I'm tired, and it's the middle of the night.' Realising it wasn't an emergency Rose laid back down and turned over.

Darren wasn't going to let it go, he kept rocking and shaking her until she'd woken up properly. He wouldn't leave her alone until he had his answers.

Rose finally opened her eyes.

'I don't understand what's going on here or what you're talking about, you're all mixed up and I need to go for a pee.'

She stormed off to the bathroom but as she made her way down the stairs Darren was hot on her heels. Panic had fully set in and she knew instinctively she needed to get out of the house, so she bypassed the bathroom and headed to the hallway.

'I thought you needed the loo?' Darren was seconds behind her and Rose was rushing to slip her shoes on and grab her coat, she couldn't get away from feeling like he was chasing her and needed to escape.

'Well, that's immature... aren't you going to talk?... for fuck's sake, won't you just say something!'

The front door slammed, thanks to the adrenaline coursing through her, Rose had managed to get out while he struggled to get his trainers on.

As she walked down the street, her mind was racing, why had she felt so afraid? What on earth was wrong with him? Were they his footsteps? Why can't he just leave me alone?

The adrenaline turned to frustration and anger as she heard the intensity of his footsteps building and she started walking faster while Darren was doing the same; he wasn't going to let this lie.

A passage between some houses gave Rose the chance to lose him for a moment, if I could get to the end and hide around the corner until he goes past, then I can take a moment to have a breather.

She wasn't that lucky, she never had been. No sooner had she stopped than she heard his footsteps again. Leaning against the wall trying to catch her breath, the realisation she was practically living a horror movie dawned on her. Wheezing as her asthma kicked in, Rose panicked.

Her inhaler was in the bathroom.

With no energy left, Darren soon caught up with her, grabbed her wrists and pushing them over her head he pinned her against the wall.

'*Why* won't you just fucking listen to me?'

Terrified, Rose tried her best to hold it together, blinking back the tears stinging her eyes, pushing down the rising panic, and trying to control her breathing, she was struggling to reclaim a grasp on reality.

'Now you've made me look like I'm the one in the wrong when it was you! It's all you! I just wanted you to listen, but you wouldn't, you were stubborn. If you'd listened, you'd see I'm just doing this because I love you so much and just want to spend time with you.'

Rose could feel her wrists throb as Darren's hands still gripped them up against the wall. Ideas were racing through her mind on how she could get out of the situation. Was it worth the struggle to try to break free? What would his reaction be? How the hell was this going on? Rose's throat was dry, and she couldn't control her breathing any longer.

'Well? Are you going to listen to me? Don't you realise what you've done?' Darren spat at her.

Then it hit her how to calm Darren down – feed him what he wanted – but she was going to have to look convincing, she had to believe she was in the wrong; she let her tears fill her eyes as she looked straight into his eyes.

'I'm sorry, I know it was me, but I was so tired, and I wasn't thinking straight.' Rose sighed as the tears fell. 'I don't seem to be getting anything right at the moment, but I'm trying my best for you, I really am.'

Rose felt his grip on her loosen and after a moment as Darren took in what she'd said, she could almost see the light switch moment when it flicked in Darren.

'See, I knew you knew it was you; don't worry. I'll forget about this, let's just get out of this rain and get home.' Den her hands and brought his forehead down and pressed it gently against hers.

'What am I going to do with you, eh, beautiful?' He gave her a kiss on the lips and rubbed his nose against hers as he guided her back towards their street. They were drenched from head to toe in the downpour and Darren held Rose's hand lovingly and pulled her in close she placed her arm across his waist.

She had to be a good girl.

* * *

As time passed, Darren delighted in these midnight disruptions, he liked to keep Rose on her toes and try to catch her out in a non-existent lie while she was still half asleep.

Pregnancy hormones were now playing havoc with her emotions and one night, while having one of those amazing, lifelike dreams about her ex coming and whisking her away and rescuing her, she was woken again.

'So, were you going to tell me?' Darren was shaking Rose and repeating his question over and over again. Shocked by the intrusion on such a dream, it took her a moment longer than normal to wake up and realise what was going on. She'd learnt her lesson about how nights like could go and was quick to start the process she thought she'd mastered.

'I'm going to pee myself, hang on,' she said and escaping his grip, she rushed to the bathroom and leapt onto the toilet hoping he realised it was a legitimate excuse with her bump being so big now. She'd grabbed her phone off the bedside counter on the way and saw that it was just after 2.00 a.m.

'So, were you going to tell me, then?' Darren asked. He always followed her when he was in this mood. There was no privacy, no personal space, where she went, he followed.

'I don't know what you're talking about, babe? But I'm on the loo here.' She wracked her brains on what his problem could be but the reasons he'd ended up like this in the past were so random and varied it could be anything from too much milk in his brew to her supposedly letting a man look at her wrong. Because she could control that!

'Don't act like you don't know when I know you do.'

Realising he wasn't going to leave her to finish in peace she cleaned up, feeling embarrassed by the lack of respect and privacy. After washing and drying her hands, she went to leave the bathroom, but Darren had other ideas. He put his arm across her chest, so she couldn't pass him.

Rose was used to walking on egg shells around him, he had become like a ticking time bomb that could explode at any time, but this was a whole new level of fear she felt.

This time she was pregnant. This time he was her husband. There was no easy way out.

Turning around back to the sink Rose could sense Darren's confused and distressed state, he was talking to himself as if he was running through various scenarios in his head. With his focus off her, she glanced at her phone and thought, *shall I chance it?*

Her heart was racing, and she was starting to get clammy. What *was he really capable of?* she thought. This wasn't the Darren she'd first met.

Darren gathered his thoughts together and screamed back to Rose, '*Well?*' He'd obviously decided she knew what he was angry about, but she still didn't have any idea.

'I'll give you a clue: you don't learn from your mistakes.' His agitation growing by the second.

'Did I not talk to you about something?' Rose replied the guess, thinking this could cover all bases but her voice gave away just how scared she was; she had no control over the tremor?

'*Why* are you doing this?! Don't *you know what's wrong?* Don't act stupid about it.'

Still undecided about trying to contact someone, Rose began humming a song in her head while he continued to scream and shout at her. She'd done this when she was a teenager and she was in trouble with her parents or teachers. It seemed childish, but it worked and helped her control her breathing. When he seemed to be losing steam, Rose saw her chance to try to calm him down like she had in the passage a few months before.

'Look, like I said, it's really late and I'm not thinking straight, you know what I'm like when I first wake up.' She spoke softly to try to calm him down. 'Can you let me know what it is I've said or done, just so I'm clear, not that I don't know – it's just so I know how I can make it right.' Darren was listening to her and let Rose continue what she was saying. 'Let me just give my dad a ring 'cause he's good at putting me in my place and I've clearly upset you, and you know that's the last thing I want to do.'

'What, so you can put me down? *I don't think so!*' Darren erupted and held his head in his hands and began pacing around near the door.

Rose realised her exit was now blocked, it was as if he was having a mental breakdown. Rose hadn't seen him behave like this before and was becoming increasingly worried about what would happen next. He wasn't as irate the last time he'd an issue with her, but it was the talking to himself Rose was concerned about. He was pacing and muttering and mumbling to himself and Rose felt the terror rise through her whole body, this was nothing like she'd ever before.

It was now or never, she knew they needed help and they needed it now. She grasped her phone in her pocket and her hand working on autopilot, she managed to get the screen unlocked before muscle memory kicked in and she located her dad's number, giving the screen a quick glance to check she had the right number while Darren paced the hallway, she managed to hit the call button.

Like a lion chasing its prey, Darren's head snapped towards her when he heard the muffled sound of the phone ringing. Gripping hold of the phone as hard as she could, Rose tried to keep it away from him as they grappled around the bathroom. Concern for her baby coursed through Rose's veins and she eventually released her grip allowing Darren to take the phone which he threw to the floor, a demonic grin on his face as it shattered apart.

Certain that would be the end of the fight, Rose barely had a chance to notice the taut, white knuckles of his clenched fist as it flew towards her.

CHAPTER THREE

Darren's clenched fist flew at her with all his anger behind it, but Rose watched it in slow motion. It wasn't the first time this had happened, but Rose still couldn't move, she was frozen to the spot. Closing her eyes tight she tried to pretend it wasn't happening… that it would all go away.

There was a crash followed by shattering glass and a moan from Darren – not what Rose was expecting. Too scared to open her eyes and find out why she wasn't hurting, Rose realised this would be a good time to escape and forced open her eyes and started to run out of the bathroom, but Darren grabbed her dressing gown and pulled her back. There was blood everywhere, red running down his arm and covering Rose, it was all over the glass and bathroom floor.

'Oh shit!' Rose grabbed a towel and quickly wrapped it around Darren's bleeding arm. She didn't know why she was helping him, but he wasn't saying anything and still looked pissed off.

'I'm going to ring for an ambulance.' Rose said as panic took over, and she rushed off to get Darren sorted, the towel was now saturated in blood and he looked pale and queasy.

The smell of iron from the blood flooded over Rose and she felt nauseous. Getting through to a 999-operator seemed to take forever and when the someone eventually answered the phone, Rose spluttered everything out so fast that it didn't give the lady a chance to speak.

The operator managed to interrupt Rose, who was practically hyperventilating and stopped her from continuing.

'OK, I've sent an ambulance but stay on the phone with me until it arrives.' She sounded like she had a peg pinned to her nose, Rose let out a huge sigh of relief; she didn't want to be on her own in this situation any longer. Rose had never felt so alone. She didn't care who would be there with her as long as someone was.

The operator continued, 'Now, what happened?'

Rose knew what she was doing, she was trying to defuse the situation but also find out if Rose was OK, in a slightly parental way. Rose hadn't realised they'd want the whole story, and it was like there was a spotlight on her, but she couldn't risk telling the real story, what if Darren heard?

'Well, you see it was all my fault.' Rose didn't sound convincing at all. 'We had an argument and I let it go too far.'

The operator said, 'Do you need the police to come over?' By now the tears were falling uncontrollably, her nose was running, and she was spluttering.

'All you have to do is say *yes* or *no* to me.' The operator understood what was going on and Rose couldn't believe it. She managed to whisper yes nervously, but she knew there would be some safety for her soon. The operator had simply listened to her; no one had done that for a very long time – this was the first time Rose recognised something was drastically wrong, and she needed help.

'The ambulance will be there any moment now, so don't

worry.' Rose grabbed an old tissue from the pocket of her dressing gown and used it to mop up her nose.

Darren was still sitting on the tiled floor, holding his arm, and mumbling something about needing a fag. Suddenly there were three loud thuds on the door; they'd arrived. Rose let out a huge sigh – she'd never felt so relieved in all her life.

It seemed like hours had passed since the phone call was made. The ambulance crew were friendly towards Rose as they came in to the house and began their job. By the time the police arrived, the paramedics were taking large pieces of glass out of Darren's arm.

Clearly not happy with Darren, they made no eye contact with him and Rose worried they'd been told she'd asked for the police and Darren might pick up on it being her fault they were there. Rose went and sat in the front room and left the paramedics to do their work. Silent tears fell as she stared into space; she could only see her life in tunnel vision and it seemed bleak. The police officer snapped Rose out of her trance,

'Are you OK dear?' she asked.

'Err, yes, why wouldn't I be OK? It's just all the blood and Darren's arm has got to me, it makes me feel sick, if you know what I mean?' Rose came up with an excuse and was confident it would pass.

'I think I know what you mean. Don't worry. I'll sit with you for a while, is that OK?'

'Of course, it is, yes, sit down of course.' The police officer sat with her while she calmed down and while the ambulance staff did their job.

The police were polite towards Rose in offering reassurance; they were stern with Darren and Rose only imagined that this would come to bite her bitterly for years to come.

That night, Darren received a verbal warning and told him to buck his ideas up. Rose was seven months pregnant so there was the baby to think about too. The other officer gave Rose a small leaflet when Darren wasn't looking. She knew exactly what it was going to say, but she wasn't going through that, *couples have arguments like this all the time, right?* Rose thought it was a little patronising, but the police were there to help so she remained quiet.

'Let's not add any stress onto her,' the police officer told Darren – it seemed like she was trying to drill the words into his skull.

Rose feared her warnings were only going to make it worse in the long run, and she wished she had telepathic powers because then she'd be able to tell them everything.

* * *

It had just been a month since the police and ambulance crew were there, and the house was becoming tarnished with unsettling memories. Darren was left with big, deep scars down his arm and even some smaller ones on his face, but they hadn't bothered him.

Rose was now eight months pregnant and had arranged to meet with her older sister, Scarlett, for the day in Leeds. Scarlett had practically brought Rose up, and she had looked up to her all their lives. Rose needed the family medical history for her midwife and was using it as an excuse to get out for the day.

Getting ready to set off for a day of shopping and gossip, Rose was running from the bathroom to the bedroom and rushing around: shower, hair, matching clothes, make-up. Darren lay in bed having a cigarette and a mug of coffee, observing her with a slight squint. She'd felt his eyes on her all morning and knew from the way he was behaving that he wasn't going to allow her to go out as planned. The atmosphere and his piercing stare were foreboding.

I will be out of the house soon enough and I will have a bit of freedom and some time to breathe, she thought.

'You look nice,' Den said as she was putting on her shoes.

'Aww, thank you,' Rose replied with a flush of pink in her cheeks, anxiety starting to trickle through her body.

'So, why did Scarlett want to meet you without me?' There was a pause, Rose had no idea how to respond. 'Or was it your idea?'

Rose realised where this was going.

'Oh, it was her idea; I think it's nice. We haven't seen each other in so long. It's nothing to do with not wanting you there, in fact, we're planning to meet again soon with you there, which will be nice, won't it?'

Darren was deep in thought and Rose could tell he was trying to work out if she was lying; he thought he could read her like a book, but he couldn't be more wrong.

'Oh right, I just think it's odd that's all.' There was another pause as he took a drag from his cigarette and slowly exhaled.

'Well, I better be getting off, I don't want to miss my train.' Rose spoke with more caution and kept her head down. The switch had been flicked in Darren once again; it had become a lot more sensitive recently and Rose didn't have to do much to trigger it, despite her best attempts to avoid it. Nothing she did was right and as much as she tried to correct her 'mistakes', she was always wrong.

'You're going to be talking about me, aren't you?' his voice raised. It was almost like a test each time he asked a question; he was waiting to analyse the results and see what he was going to ask next, the problem being it was always going to end his way. 'Why am I having to sit here all day on my day off while you talk about me to your *precious* sister?' He was winding himself up. Rose didn't know what to do when he started being this way, so she cowered and spoke back quietly.

'You know that's not true, I love you, we're just talking about the medical stuff.'

Wrong answer she realised almost immediately. That was all the ammunition he needed.

'So, don't you think I should be there? It's my baby too! Unless there's something you have to tell me?'

Rose knew exactly what he was trying to imply, and she nearly laughed at the utter ridiculousness of it. She rarely left his side; she never went out with her friends anymore so what possible chance had she had to have sex with anyone else?

A firm response would be a good call, she thought, tweaking how she handled him, because even though she knew she'd have to give in in the end, it was still worth being able to have some sort of voice and see if there was a chance that she could smooth things over.

'Well, that's not possible; I'm with you and love you; what reason would I have to do that? I'm just going to see my sister, have lunch, and do some shopping. It's completely harmless.' Rose had become very familiar with this pattern of behaviour and knew the guilt trip came next.

'If you *loved* me, I would be coming with you.' Darren stood up and out of nowhere threw his half-empty cup of coffee at her. It smashed against the wall just an inch away from her face; a couple of shards sliced the left side of her cheek. Rose didn't flinch, she simply held her face with one hand to stop the little bleeding.

Looking down she saw that the mug was one her father

had given her when she was a teenager, *yet again something of mine.* It read 'Daddy's little girl forever' on it.

Tears pricked her eyes, but she managed to overcome the emotion and speak, 'Why are you doing this? I've said I love you. That was my mug you've broken, and it meant something to me.'

'Well, you shouldn't have given me a reason. If you go on your own, then don't come back.' Always quick to answer, Darren was able to turn the situation around so that it was her fault.

Rose felt like she was being locked up in a prison cell and he was throwing away the key; the happy day she'd planned was now ruined – he'd be coming with her.

She would have to watch what she said for the rest of the day, she was used to watching her body language in case any slight glance or smirk set him off and she was getting better at being an emotionless robot lately, it was almost a state of mind to protect herself from the reality of what was happening around her.

'The train goes in twenty-five minutes, so we have to leave in five,' Rose said bluntly as she left the room to go downstairs and wait for Darren there.

He'd spend the whole time complaining that he was bored looking around the shops, he always did, but Rose waited for him and sure enough, he came down and led the way out the door like he was her bodyguard. She couldn't go anywhere in public without him being more than a couple of meters away from her anymore.

They walked to the train station in silence, Rose felt nothing but resent towards him and she wanted to scream and be released from the leash; thank goodness she had learnt to fake a smile.

CHAPTER FOUR

Scarlett knew there was something wrong, Rose could tell. The atmosphere was uncomfortable, and Darren was acting so far from normal it was bizarre to watch. He was acting too smooth, laughing at Scarlett's jokes, and relishing the attention from these sisters and soaking up the envious looks he was getting from the men around them. He had never been this down to earth around Scarlett before and it stuck out like a sore thumb.

Unable to enjoy her time, Rose had to watch every word she spoke, she now recognised the moments she needed to tighten up her 'loose tongue'. She knew that for every glance a man made towards her, as much as Darren was enjoying it at the time, she'd pay for it later.

She spent most of the day trying to tell Scarlett telepathically what was going on, but it was like screaming in a soundproof room or being stuck in a horrible dream and wanting to get out.

He didn't leave them alone long enough for them to catch up properly, and when she got home, Rose sobbed into her pillow at how her life was falling apart around her.

Before long, she barely spoke with her friends or family. They were sick of hearing about the fall outs and then when Rose informed them that he'd made a miraculous change, her fake smiles and pretence were obvious. Her weekly phone call with Scarlett stopped and she'd become isolated but Darren's family were nearby, and she was able to see and speak with them without much fallout from him, so that made life a little easier for her.

Darren's mum, Joan, was a short lady with hair bleached so blonde it was almost white and got on with her surprisingly well. She often visited her in the afternoons and they'd watch *Come Dine With Me* together over a cuppa and a biscuit. Rose knew that with her first baby on the way it was important to try to keep the family on side and for them to be in her child's life.

Towards the end of the pregnancy, Darren was doing some decorating ready for the arrival of their baby and his thirteen-year-old sister, Katie, had offered to help. Rose Decided to go to his mum's get out of the way and, after a couple of hours, she was tired and decided to walk home.

Katie had already left, and Darren was finishing up the room, so she decided to put her feet up and watch some rubbish TV and she fell asleep almost instantly all cosy under the throw.

A few days passed, and Darren was taking Rose out for a meal, when she discovered a locket out of her jewellery box wasn't in its rightful place. 'Darren… Darren…' Rose was trying to get him to hear her despite him being downstairs and with the TV blaring away. 'DARREN!' Pregnancy hormones had given her a new lease of rage, well, Darren called it rage, she called it being assertive when she dared!

Darren paused the Sky TV as if it was an inconvenience she'd even spoken to him.

'My locket isn't there… have you seen it?'

'Why would I have seen it? You know what you're like at losing things. It's probably somewhere else.'

Rose was getting grumpier as she wanted some help in finding it, feeling worried as to where it had gone.

'Well, can you help me look for it?' And with great annoyance Darren started hunting round the house with her but with no joy.

Days passed, and it didn't turn up and although Rose was one for misplacing things, not something as precious as this locket; it was her aunt's, the same aunt had given her the now smashed mirror. It was expensive, and above all, held great sentimental value to her. There was something about Darren's reaction this whole thing that made Rose suspicious, but she couldn't place her finger on what.

Another few days passed, and Darren was on the phone to his mum; Katie had been taken down to the police station for shoplifting. Rose couldn't believe it but then the penny dropped. Katie had been in the house just a week ago. The day her locket disappeared. Could she have taken it? Did Darren know? Is that why he'd been a little keener than he would normally be when helping her to look for it? Surely, not?

How on earth was I going to bring this up? Rose thought as she listened in on the conversation, but as soon as he got off the phone, she couldn't hold back.

'Den, I overheard a bit of that… is everything all right?'

Darren didn't hesitate to respond, 'Not really, bloody Katie again upsetting Mum because of her childish decisions; she's down the police station because the shop caught her stealing.'

Rose was a little concerned for his mum as she did get on with Joan. 'Oh, no… is your mum OK?'

'She will be; she's used to it, but it doesn't stop me from being annoyed.'

'I know now isn't the best time, but I need to say it... I think Katie took the locket.' Darren shifted a look her way and was about to interrupt. 'Because... Well, because she was here that day helping you and then my locket goes missing...'

Rose braced herself for the argument that was bound to follow but Darren wasn't even angry, and he just replied, 'Oh, well... I was going to talk to you about that.'

'Talk to me about what?'

'Well, you know you're always getting on with my mum, you're amazing like that; you know I'm really lucky to have you because my family is a mess and you accept them for who they are.' Rose wasn't buying what he had to say, it was like he was trying to fluff her up with compliments and she looked at him with a blank expression. 'My mum needed some money and Katie was looking through your jewellery box and I said it was worth something.'

Not fully processing what he had said, Rose felt the panic rising through her body, her breath coming in short, sharp bursts. 'Not that it means something to me? Not that my dead aunt gave me it? You didn't tell her those things? Just that it was worth money? How dare you let her look through my things?' She couldn't explain the anger, the upset, the disappointment, and the betrayal she felt if she could try. Trying to calm down she continued, 'And you just *let* her take it?'

'No, no, no... I wasn't there, she took it, but she did tell me a few days later when I mentioned it had gone missing.'

Rose was sweating, she was hot with rage; no care, no feelings, no sympathy, no empathy, no nothing! 'So why didn't you tell me?'

'Because I didn't want you to change your opinion of my family,' Darren replied.

Use my good will against me and then say my good will isn't good enough! Rose stormed off to her bedroom and screamed and cried into the pillow, and by the time went back downstairs, Darren had gone to work.

Not even an apology.

* * *

The moment Rose set eyes on her baby girl she felt an instant love and need to protect her. She promised her tiny daughter that she was going to keep her safe.

Rose had always wanted to be a mum, in fact since she was ten when she got to meet a family friend's baby, she spent the whole afternoon holding it and marvelling at its perfect features and how it needed someone to look after it all the time. Rose had always felt there was something missing in her life but that stopped the second her daughter was placed in her arms for the first time.

Darren was great during the first week after Millie-Rose arrived. He looked after them both so well, Rose was more than a little shocked at how smitten he was with them.

The only issue they'd had was that the hospital took their baby photo's outside of visiting hours so only Rose's hand was visible holding the baby. Darren wasn't happy at all when he found out and Rose expected him to kick off with the staff, but she managed to placate him by taking some on her phone. They weren't as good quality as those the professional had taken, but Darren seemed happy and that's all that mattered.

They settled into a routine once home and Rose felt the closest to content she had for a long time.

Millie-Rose was two-months-old when they went into town to open her a savings account and it suddenly started pouring with rain. They dashed into Starbucks, which was the nearest option for cover. It was darker than normal inside due to the weather change, it was quite eerie. As they were queuing for drinks, Millie-Rose woke up and wasn't happy at all. Rose manoeuvred the pram over to a window seat so that she could comfort her and feed her as she was getting hungry.

Getting settled with her dripping wet hair hanging over her face, Rose's anxiety shot through the roof as she realised this would be her first time breast feeding in public. People were already looking at her following her attempts at getting the pram through the tables, then the baby crying, now she had to try to get Millie-Rose latched on quickly, so she could get her to stop crying.

The eerie lighting, the unfamiliar surroundings, and an anxious mummy did nothing to calm Millie-Rose though, and she didn't latch on. Then, just as she was about to settle, Rose saw Darren coming over with their drinks, his face more thunderous than the sky outside.

'Flash your fucking tits to the whole shop why you don't you!' he hissed at her as he sat down.

Feeling like she'd be slapped, Rose couldn't believe what he was saying. He continued to tell her she was a selfish cow for breast feeding and stopping him bonding with his daughter. He didn't care about any of the other things a father could do to bond with his child, he thought Rose was lazy as she got to sit with her feet up while she fed her. He wasn't interested in changing nappies, bathing her, playing with her toys, this was all about control, Rose realised. This was one part of her life he had no control over at all.

As she tuned out of his ranting, she heard him muttering about changing her to formula milk.

* * *

Millie-Rose is now eighteen months old and Rose was more concerned than usual about things with Darren. Normally around her constantly, watching her every move, recently he had seemed distant. Staying out until the early hours after work, head stuck in his phone all the time. She couldn't shake the feeling that something wasn't right.

One morning she was playing afternoon tea, shops, doctors, and chefs with Millie-Rose. Her hair had grown long enough to be able to French-plait it; Rose's aunt had always braided her hair when she was younger, and she used to love getting it done up and adding daisies to it. It warmed her heart to do Millie-Rose's just like hers used to be.

After recently finding out she was pregnant again, Rose was feeling queasy and took some time out from their games on the sofa. She knew she was expecting a boy this time, she'd convinced Darren to find out so that they could be better prepared with the things they'd need to buy if it was a boy, or what they could reuse if it was a girl. She'd chosen to name their baby boy Harrison.

As she lay waiting for the nausea to pass, she took out her phone and went to check her Facebook. It was still signed in to Darren's account as he preferred to use her Internet allowance at home, so he could save his for when he was out. He also wanted her to have less access to the outside world, she wasn't stupid not to know that was the main reason, although he never said it. Hit with a sudden craving, Rose went to grab the pickled onions and a bar of marzipan from the kitchen when a name in Darren's messages list made her stop. She didn't recognise this girl's name so clicked her image through to her profile.

Claire Thornby had a profile picture showing off her very

generous cleavage and a lovely slim figure and Rose felt instantly that she should be cautious. She clicked back into the inbox and scrolled up – to find out that they'd been chatting a lot. Rose didn't need to read much because when she read the lines, *I had fun last night… I loved you in that bikini, you looked amazing,* and her replies, *you really had your way with me… when are we meeting up again?* Rose knew exactly what he'd done; he'd cheated on her and her gut was telling her that this wasn't the first time.

Anger, frustration, and nausea rocked her all at the same time; she couldn't understand why he'd do this. He went on and on about Rose not being able to go out alone because he was worried other men would come onto her and that Rose wouldn't say no she realised now he thought this way because he was up to no good, he thought she was too!

Infuriated with herself because he'd treated her like a stereotypical 1950s housewife and had she'd obliged thinking he had issues he didn't know how to control. Sitting there with her phone in her hand, Rose felt completely stupid, humiliated, embarrassed, and ashamed.

What would my family and friends think?

Who have I got to help me?

They'll all say that they knew this would happen to me and that I should have listened.

Rose felt hot, cold, shaky, angry, happy, distraught, and overwhelmed. Rose felt alone in this and questioned what she could do as she was expecting their second child. If he found out she knew, he wouldn't be bothered. He wouldn't display any guilt or regret or sorrow. He was carefree and if he did care, even a tiny jot, he had a good way of hiding it.

She needed to get out of the house. She needed some time to figure out what she was going to do. She got Millie ready, and they headed off in the car, Millie singing away in

34

the back seat and Rose just driving. Eventually, she had to pull over and throw up at the side of the road. She was in complete turmoil.

Parking up outside York city centre, she decided to walk the rest of the way to the shops and take Mille for a treat of tiffin and hot chocolate at Costa Coffee.

Millie-Rose was in her pushchair making a huge mess out of a tiny bit of this treat, but Rose was thankful for the time to distract her mind and detract from the urge to break down in tears. Rose felt like a failure and a bad parent, *but it wasn't my fault!* she kept reassuring herself to instil some confidence.

I know that the person I was before meeting Darren wouldn't have taken any of this shit and would've left him straight away, but the question now was, how on earth was I going to leave him without it being difficult? Where was I going to go? How would I cope when I was pregnant? How could I cope financially? I already knew I was trapped in a corner and there was no easy way out. If there was, it certainly wasn't clear, and it would mean going through a lot of stress and not just the usual stresses of a break-up but the added fear of what he might do if we did break-up.

Millie-Rose was now showing her creative side by drawing pictures in her chocolate-spit mess on the table. All the while, Rose was having an internal battle. She kept asking herself the questions – Could she let this go over her head? Could she pretend she didn't know? Could she carry on? But the answer to each question was a big fat no.

Rose couldn't help but plot out a dramatic solution in her head – getting her hair dyed and chopped off and be unrecognisable so she could escape Darren, rush off, and start a new happy life; that would be nice, but she stopped these thoughts because she knew she wouldn't get far before he'd track her down.

There were so many reasons why Rose had to stay; it was depressing and degrading for her.

Reading over some of the messages again and she felt so angry she was suffering for no reason; he'd put her through some crazy crap and accused her of having affairs God knows how many times, when in fact it was him playing away. She also knew if she mentioned it to him he'd somehow turn it around and make it her fault and blame her for his actions.

Rose was getting upset again and so she cleaned up Millie-Rose and they set off for another walk. They headed down The Shambles, a little real-life Diagon Alley from *Harry Potter* style street made up of crooked slanting houses which always cheered her up. Rose loved to see the tourists taking selfies down this street, it has a magical feeling as well as like a piece of architectural art.

Rose had been walking aimlessly with Millie-Rose for a couple of hours when Darren texted to ask where they were. She didn't answer. She didn't know how to, and her silence spoke the words to him. Millie-Rose was nagging for a drink, so they popped into the newsagents and bought her a blackcurrant Fruit Shoot, some crisps, a chocolate bar, and some Paracetamol for Rose as she had a stinking headache.

They continued to walk around, and they enjoyed the sun, nipped for a swing in the park and looked at the children's DVDs in an entertainment shop. If Rose was honest with herself, she didn't want to go home at all; she wanted to ride away and find happiness with her little girl and baby.

It started to get cold and Rose was getting tired from the walking so they headed back to the car.

They soon got settled in the car and Rose had her shopping on the passenger seat and she ate the chocolate bar as the tears fell once again, chocolate couldn't make this better for her; hiding her tears was hard even when she had a beautiful girl smiling at her in the rear-view mirror. Millie-Rose finished her Fruit Shoot and now wanted something to eat. Rose got her crisps out of the bag and handed them to her, a bit of a junk food kind of day but had a great excuse. She then noticed the Paracetamol out of the corner of her eye and paused. Rose opened both packets and one by one, in no time at all, she swallowed them all. Rose didn't know what she was thinking at first but once they were gone, she knew exactly what she was thinking.

I could end this misery for good, I could be out from under his control, I could be free, and I feel happy about it.

She sat waiting, thinking something would happen instantly, thinking she wouldn't have time to regret her decision. Looking back at her beautiful daughter she burst into tears again.

What about her, Rose thought? What life would Rose be leaving for her?

She wouldn't get the upbringing Rose wanted for her and she deserved the best. Millie-Rose started to ask, 'Why you cry, Mummy? It OK, Mummy? Love you.' She was speaking in her cute, high-pitched babbly voice.

Rose had never felt so guilty and so trapped, she couldn't end this even if she wanted to. She couldn't end her own life, she needed to stay to make sure Millie-Rose was protected and to make sure she had the best of a bad situation, a diabolical and desperately bad situation.

She couldn't control the floods of tears that came as she thought about her future and what it would be like without her. What would Millie-Rose become? Rose felt like a bad mother having brought her into the life they were living.

The reality of what had just happened hit and Rose knew

she needed to get the drugs out of her system and fast. It didn't matter that she was parked on a busy street near the city centre, it didn't matter what she had to do. She rammed her fingers down her throat, out of Millie-Rose's sight, and opened the car door... it didn't take long, and Rose had managed to make myself sick, but it was a painful, acidic bile came up because all she'd eaten was one chocolate bar and a smidge of chocolate tiffin.

Rose couldn't chance it and kept making herself sick until there was nothing left; *what about the baby?* Rose couldn't think of anything else while upset and only now did she consider the consequences of her actions. *I'm not a cruel and horrible person.* Rose felt stupid and immature to even think of doing something like this.

Her sick was splattered all over the pavement next to the car. There were no passers-by but even if there had been, Rose wouldn't have cared. She felt she'd let him win for a moment, this is what he wanted – to push her over the edge – Rose vowed she wouldn't let him take over her like that again.

After just five minutes of emptying her stomach, Rose walked around to Millie-Rose's side of the car, opened her door, hugged her, and gave her a kiss and said, 'I love you so much you know, I'm never going to leave you, *ever.*'

Rose made her that promise there and then. It made her realise that she needed to train herself not to be bothered by Darren because she couldn't get into this state again. There was no way she'd ever leave her Millie-Rose in this mess. Rose thought she'd feel resentful of her, but she didn't; she was giving her the strength to carry on and the focus she needed to train herself.

Thinking about it further, Rose was hurt, upset, and angry over the love she once had for Darren. Concentrating on herself and the kids was going to be the way forwards, putting her own feelings aside for the time being wouldn't be a bad decision. Feeling empowered to live for her children and not be ruled by Den, even if he thought he was clever in what he was doing, Rose knew she could try to be one step ahead and think like she knew the game and what he was doing.

Could she manage it?

CHAPTER FIVE

Walking through the door later that day, Rose had no idea what she was going to do or say when she saw Darren but the look on his face told her she was in trouble.

'Got something to tell me?' he asked.

Rose froze.

'Been snooping have you, bitch?' His face was full of thunder and Rose had never been so terrified, the turmoil of the day was still raw.

'What do you mean?' she asked tentatively.

'Don't think I don't know what you've been doing. Do you think I'm bothered that you know? Do you think it'll make me stop?'

'Den, I need to get Mille-Rose her tea, and I'm shattered, we've been out all day. What do you fancy? I was gonna go to the chippy...'

'Fuck that! I'm going out. I'm off to see a proper woman!'

'You're not going to deny it then?' Rose's resolve not to break down failed her miserably.

'What's the point? It's your fault. If you put out like a wife should I wouldn't have to look for it elsewhere, would I? You bring these things on yourself you do, Rose. Don't dare start with me! She's more of a woman than you'll ever be.'

Darren grabbed his coat from the hook in the hallway and went to open the door.

'Fish fucking supper,' he sneered, 'I'm off to get a home-cooked meal from a real woman.'

And he slammed the door behind him.

'Where Daddy go, Mummy?' Millie-Rose looked up at Rose with a combination of fear and confusion.

Not sure what to say or do, Rose gathered up her baby girl, took her upstairs, and snuggled into bed with her. They put *Beauty and the Beast* on and after they'd picked at the takeaway Rose ordered, Mille-Rose finally drifted off to sleep.

Rose barely caught a wink that night. For all his faults Den was her husband. He was the father of her children. How was she going to cope without him? What would she do when the baby arrived? Folding her free arm around her bump, she wept, she wept for hours that night, torn between love and hate; hate and love. For Darren.

But mostly hate for herself.

* * *

When she woke the next morning, shocked that she'd managed to sleep at all, it was to the smell of bacon and eggs.

She could hear noises coming from downstairs and the radio was playing. When she walked into the kitchen, she found Darren wearing her Cath Kidston apron; he handed her a cup of tea, kissed her on the cheek, and turned back to the stove where he had a full English breakfast on the go.

Rose sat down, too stunned for words.

'Look, babe,' he said, not looking at her. 'You shouldn't have snooped, you shouldn't have read my messages, I knew you had because the last one she sent, I'd been saving to read alone, and well... you opened it... that can't have been nice. But look, it's not right is it? I'm a married man and I don't get none. The lads take the piss. She was there, offering it, no strings.'

The penny dropped. Darren had gone to his bit on the side last night and she'd told him to do one. She didn't want the hassle of a married man with a toddler and a kid on the way. She looked at his back, eyes firing daggers at him.

'Rose, darling, all you gotta do is show your husband you love him. You get that, don't ya?'

Almost choking on her tea, Rose said, 'Of course, darling. Thanks for the brew.'

She knew. She knew what was going to come. He was going to be the doting husband and she was going to milk it. She had no choice until she figured a way out of this mess.

* * *

Weeks passed, and as Rose suspected he would, Darren changed. He'd made an effort and it was the most he'd done for her since they'd got together.

Rose had enjoyed the extra work he'd been putting in: making meals, doing a spot of cleaning, being good with the children, being the man Rose thought she'd married – the person she'd originally met.

Why can't he be like this all the time? Why does he suddenly change? What do I do that's so wrong?

Rose couldn't help but question her own actions and blaming herself.

Maybe I need to be calmer? Maybe I need to be aware of what I am doing and saying? Maybe I need to be more irresistible to him, so he won't get distracted?

As the weeks passed, she could feel the honeymoon period was about to end, but she'd not expected in the first place, so she couldn't complain.

Then Harrison came into the world and took everyone by surprise as he was a big baby, in fact he was almost double the size of the baby in the next bed.

Big or not, Rose was besotted with her little man, he took to her breast so naturally and impressed the all midwifes on the ward. It seemed easier the second time round; Rose knew what to expect as she'd done it once before. She grew in confidence as time passed and the health visitors continued to her praise her and the children's development.

She took the compliments where she could nowadays.

* * *

Harrison was thriving at five-months-old and Rose received praise from the Health Visitor each time she came to check up on him and Millie-Rose.

Still shocked at how things had turned out, Rose was happy in their new house. They'd had to leave their old two-up, two-down in a hurry and, as she was pregnant at the time, they'd managed to secure a three-bed terrace near to Darren's family.

She was feeding Harrison one morning when Millie-Rose needed to go to the toilet, she asked Darren to take her up.

Darren knew it would be difficult for Rose to take her while Harrison was latched on, but he still gave her the *stare*, the one which Rose told her she was already on thin ice as she hadn't got round to hoovering or doing any of the other household chores. Darren liked Rose to be on top of the housework and for the house to be clean and tidy, he didn't like things out of place. He also didn't like helping.

Millie-Rose went up to the bathroom and was singing away as she took her time on the toilet. Rose could hear Darren's heavy sighs from downstairs. It wasn't as if she'd disturbed him in the middle of an important task, he'd just been sat looking at his phone.

Millie-Rose must have started to mess about, as Darren came stomping down the stairs with her held like a rugby ball under his arm. She was screaming and kicking, and he slammed her down on the bottom step – the naughty step. Rose cringed as she heard the dull, hard thud, and knew it must have hurt her bottom. He'd slammed her down from waist height. He came back into the living room and slammed the door hard leaving Millie-Rose in the pitch-black hallway, there was no light from the front door, Millie-Rose was crying, and Rose wanted to go and comfort her, her girl was scared of the dark and was obviously afraid and in pain.

Rose had to ask, knowing what he might do to her, but she needed to know and do what mothers do best and protect her child. 'What was she doing?' she asked with a nervous giggle as she got up, went over to the door, and opened it slightly so Millie-Rose had some light from the living room to relieve her fear.

'Just the usual, using too much toilet roll,' Darren snapped back.

Rose thought this was an inadequate reason to react the way he had and felt sorry for Millie-Rose, she defended her slightly. 'Kids are kids, I guess?'

Darren gave her that stare again, and she knew she was

pushing her luck, however she struggled up as she was still feeding Harrison. Rose had become a master at walking around and doing basic tasks while still breastfeeding Harrison – she was rather proud of this, but she was given no option.

Rose went to see Millie-Rose, she pulled down her trousers and could see her red bum, it was going to bruise. She was clearly in distress and pain, Rose comforted her and couldn't care less if Darren was going to punish her for it.

Rose held Millie-Rose in her arms, she wanted to tell her she was going to take her away and keep her safe, that no matter what happened she'd be OK. But she didn't because she couldn't be sure, she wouldn't make a promise she couldn't keep.

She needed to do whatever it took to protect Millie-Rose. Rose stroked her hair, and she cuddled into her, tears filled her eyes and slid down her face; Rose had never felt as much love as she did for Millie-Rose and Harrison.

Darren was now clanging a teaspoon into his mug, banging the cupboard doors in the kitchen, and muttering to himself with the occasional grunt. Rose laughed at this in her head, how pathetic she thought. Millie-Rose is just a little girl, and he was letting her get the better of him, over the toilet!

The previous night Rose had accidentally slept through Harrison crying for his feed at around 3.00 a.m. Normally, she was in-tune like a digital radio set to one station: the parent channel. She'd woken up to the warning cry that Harrison was making, that horrible cry that babies give when there is really something wrong; the one in which a parent drops everything they are doing to attend to them.

Running into Harrison's room Rose was unsure of what was going on or what was wrong with him. Adrenaline was pumping through her as she panicked through to his bedroom. When she got there, she couldn't believe what she saw. Darren was banging his fists onto the cot mattress either side of Harrison and shouting in his face, 'Shut up, you fucking cock, what do you want? I'm trying to sleep!'

Rose pushed him out of the way and took Harrison into her arms immediately and started to cradle him to calm down his crying.

'It's OK, Mummy's here now, I need to wake up faster for you,' she whispered as she shushed and soothed him. She swung him side to side and tried to get him to latch on.

Harrison took a good five minutes to calm down from his screaming and had managed to latch on, he sobbed and took a breath with a little cry and then had a few guzzles, then sobbed and took a breath with a cry and had another few guzzles. After around twenty minutes, Rose had managed to calm him so that he was now having a full feed.

Feeling a loss that her children didn't have a dad but bully living with them instead, Rose knew then that she had better, had to be even more tuned in to her parent channel; the drop of a pin and she'd need to respond quickly. She was practically a single parent; forced to be this way to protect her children. Rose didn't mind because they were her world and they were the reason she kept living each day.

It dawned on her that it was no longer just her getting hurt, the children were now being dragged into it. That was the moment Rose lost all respect and feelings she used to have of love and friendship for Darren, they were now gone.

He now had something to complain about almost daily, there was always something she had, or hadn't, done. She'd tried to change herself to please Darren, but she never seemed to fit the mould he'd made for her. She was always in the wrong even though she did everything.

As the weeks passed, and she did more and more with less and less time for herself, she started to look pale and worn out. She knew, despite what had happened in the past when she'd this, she needed to ask for help. Food poisoning had overcome Rose, her stomach was cramping and squeezing in pain and it was empty from the vomiting. Stuck on the toilet for hours in the night as the diarrhoea was working its way through her body until there was nothing left. It was like a tap that wouldn't switch off.

Rose was clammy and sweating out the illness. She hoped and prayed that Millie-Rose and Harrison would sleep longer than usual so that she could get it out of her system and feel better. Rose soon realised she couldn't control her recovery and when morning came she was curled up in the fetal position.

Still suffering and exhausted from crawling to feed Harrison and then back to the bathroom all night, the doctors advised Rose to get some help from family if Darren couldn't take the time off work. As her family weren't available, she had no choice but to ask Darren.

'Darren…?' Rose whimpered to him while he was having his morning coffee and cig, he rolled his eyes and flicked the ash onto his tray as he heard Rose's tone of voice.

'I've spoken to my family, and no one is available to help, no one can get here, and I've tried everyone.' Rose sat down on the floor as her stomach cramped again.

'It's not my problem, is it?' Darren responded coldly.

'I'm so unwell, Den, please understand I just need some help. Just today if nothing else?' She was mortified at having to beg for help, but what was she supposed to do?

Den said nothing, and Rose hated the silent pauses because she couldn't see what he was thinking. He continued to take drags from his cigarette and swig from his oversized mug of coffee. Millie-Rose and Harrison were getting louder shouting for their mummy from their bedroom, so Rose decided to go back up to them and try to sort them out. Crawling up the stairs was easier than walking, her stomach felt like knifes were slicing through her skin. She managed to get them onto her lap and went down the stairs with them on her knee, they thought it was a ride and a bit of fun; Millie-Rose giggled all the way down and Harrison was looking up to Rose with huge smiles. Doing this biting away at the little energy she had left, every little move exhausting her, all she wanted to do was to be able to overcome it. Rose didn't want to rely on anyone else, she wanted to feel independent in her own way; never expecting anything from anyone.

'Come on then, Millie-Rose, let's sit at the table.' Den surprised her when they got downstairs, he sounded cheery and encouraging. Millie-Rose sat down, and Rose placed Harrison in his bouncer. For a moment, Rose lay on the sofa and held Harrison's hand from above, he was in such a happy mood today which made her feel a little better. Millie-Rose ate her Cheerios and Den boiled the kettle, a few minutes later he came in with a cup of tea for her.

'Thank you, you didn't have to do that.' Rose thanked Darren, she was impressed with him and glad he was helping. 'I may not be able to have it all though because everything I've had so far, I've thrown up, but you've made my day thinking of me like that. I love you.'

The temperature in the room dropped.

'You will fucking drink it because I used my energy to make you a goddamn cup of tea.' Rose couldn't bring herself to drink it even if she wanted to, she knew that moments later she'd be vomiting it up uncontrollably.

'OK,' Rose replied anxiously and gave a slight smile, letting it pass over her head.

'Well, go on…' Den pressed it.

'Oh, right, I was letting it cool for a bit.' Rose hoped she could distract him from another problem she'd caused. She took the littlest sip to prove a point and put it back on the floor.

'Being funny, are we?' Den wasn't going to leave it. Within a matter of seconds, he'd poured the tea over Rose's head and she jumped up screeching, ran straight to the bathroom to get under a cold shower as fast as she could. The pain was piercing, stinging, the cold water didn't do much to settle it before Den came in.

'You seemed to move just fine then, I was just picking it up to take to the kitchen when I slipped but I couldn't believe the reaction I saw, acting all along!' Rose couldn't make out some of what he started to come out with as the cold water tricked over her ears and down her neck, sickness swept over her and she tried to hold in the urge to throw up. 'I think you should come with me.'

Den wasn't going to give up on what he'd started.

Why don't I learn my lesson, Rose remember to never expect anything from him; she thought she shouldn't have even thought about asking.

Rose managed to get a towel over her hair and took a quick glance in the mirror, she could see the sore, bright-red face looking back at her, her skin felt like it had harsh pins and needles stabbing her scalp and face. Unable to hold it in any longer, she threw up in the toilet bowl, unsure what her next move was going to be. Retrieving a cold flannel, Rose placed it on the side of her face, the side which was sorer and went to check on Millie-Rose and Harrison. What on earth would Millie-Rose think?

'Mummy, you OK? You silly.' Millie-Rose had been briefed that Mummy had an accident.

Den was waiting for her. 'Come with me.' Rose could hear him raising his voice from the hallway.

Rose followed like his voice like a sheep follows their shepherd, she'd learnt quickly it was best not to go against his requests. Darren guided Rose to the front door and held her hand for a moment.

'It's OK, don't worry, I will have the kids today, enjoy your day.' Den opened the door and shoved Rose out, she was breathing fast and wondering what to do, her face felt like it was still burning, her top was soaking wet from the shower. In shock, she tried to control her breathing and calm herself down.

Rose was stood in front of her own home and wanted to be with the kids more than ever. Staggering around the corner, she found a wall to sit on and began sobbing while she held her face in the damp flannel, her stomach was griping, and she tried to gather her thoughts.

A little while later, Rose went around the back of the house to look through the window and check on the kids, hoping she wouldn't be seen. It was an overcast day, the sun couldn't do its job and dry or warm her, in fact she was so cold she was shivering.

Looking through the window Rose saw the kids were fine and happy and he was playing nicely with them, if only she could have seen this side of him before. Rose then walked to her friend, Lindsey's, house and spent the day there.

Lindsey didn't believe the excuse that she'd accidentally scolded herself as the tap was on the hottest setting and then she'd got caught in a flash of rain on the way over to her house. It was sickeningly obvious what Rose was covering up, but Lindsey decided to help her and spend the time looking after her.

Lindsey gave her a change of clothes, brought the thick

blankets down from upstairs and they watched chick flicks for the day. Rose managed to get some sleep and was able to go to the bathroom with a little more dignity than before. Lindsey was like a nurse to her that day and she couldn't thank Lindsey enough.

When she returned home, Den let her back in with the words, 'I hope you've learnt your lesson.' Rose simply nodded and went to see the kids who were settled and asleep, they looked peaceful and fine and that's all that mattered.

CHAPTER SIX

Exhaustion was creeping up on Rose each week she spent with Darren, it wasn't just about looking after the children but also making sure she was there before Darren when something had happened with them. Rose was trying to man manage, be on call 24/7, trying to predetermine everyone's moves and didn't have time to think about herself or her sanity.

* * *

It had been a long night of teething for Harrison and Rose must have had about three hours' worth of sleep so found it a little difficult to get up when Millie-Rose called from her room.

Giving Darren a nudge to get up considering he hadn't been any help with Harrison, she was surprised when he jumped straight out of bed. Rose couldn't help spreading out in the bed and enjoying the space... until she heard him scream at Millie-Rose.

'How dare you disrespect our house like this?'

What on earth had she done to make him scream like that? Rose thought.

'Now you can wash this up.'

Millie-Rose was only two and a half and didn't understand much and Rose knew she needed to intervene, so she got out of bed and made her way to them, thinking he was most likely doing this for a reaction out of her than taking whatever it was seriously. Harrison was now screaming, too, Darren had frightened him awake. Looking into Millie-Rose's bedroom she could see felt-tip pen daubed on the walls; Millie-Rose was in tears and walked towards her mummy.

'Have you seen this?' Darren bellowed.

'Yes, I have but I think you're a little out of tone.' Rose picked Millie-Rose up for a hug and as her little girl sobbed on her shoulder Rose's hand went hot – Millie-Rose had wet herself.

The anger Rose felt towards Darren at that moment was beyond anything she'd felt before. How could he do this to her? She had no idea that this was wrong. The guilt flooded over Rose as she remembered she hadn't taken the pens out of the bedroom yesterday.

Accidents weren't allowed to happen in Darren's house.

Darren slammed the door and walked off; annoyed Rose was comforting their distraught daughter. Rose didn't care; she bathed Millie-Rose while Harrison snuggled in his baby sling. All the while she was thinking if only she'd gone to Millie-Rose in the first place then this wouldn't have happened. *Was she really that bad for wanting a bit of sleep?*

Rose started to tell herself, sleep deprivation will not get to me... sleep deprivation will not get to me... sleep deprivation will not get to me.

When Millie-Rose had been born, she was used as a tool

to keep Rose. Rose felt like someone had locked her up and thrown away the key, she was on her own in this "family" home and Darren was non-existent as a father. If Rose was honest, she didn't mind most of the time; it was nicer when he wasn't at home, there was no walking on eggshells and Rose could be herself.

Rose felt an overprotective love for her children and it was her duty to protect them from him too, even if that meant taking a beating herself, she would do it.

Darren hardly ever hurt Rose physically but the threats and the times he had was enough for Rose to 'behave' and believe that it could lead to a lot worse. Sometimes, Rose wished he would just hit her and get it over and done with because the tension and screaming and shouting was too much for her to take. The stress was starting to take a severe toll on her now and even when the children did sleep, she couldn't.

She now knew exactly what exhaustion was.

* * *

After Harrison was born, Darren increased the pressure on Rose to lose her baby weight. Not afraid to tell her he wasn't happy with her body, he took pleasure in tormenting her about her weight and looks. Going so far as to tell her she had more roll-backs than Asda!

One afternoon, Rose had to go see the bank manager about her debts. Darren was in town with her, he wouldn't leave her side very often as he couldn't trust that she wouldn't hit on every man she saw out and about. He didn't go to the meeting; that would mean he'd have to take some responsibility for the financial mess they were in instead of palm all the responsibility on to her.

After the meeting, Rose met him outside the bank and was surprised to see he'd been shopping in Primark. He handed her a large bag filled with clothes. Rose felt emotional as he'd not done anything like this for years, she had holes in all her socks, her knickers were grey instead of white, and she'd patched her jeans so much everyone thought they were handmade. Rose wasn't sure how to respond or what to think.

Gushing her thanks, she started to look through the contents and saw a gorgeous-looking flowery top. As she pulled it out, Darren made a noise.

'Hmm, I didn't know what size you were, so I told the lass you were a bit chubby around the middle and needed to cover your belly – she said this top should do it.' Den smiled at Rose as if he was delighted.

The top was like a tent and as Rose raised her head to look at him, she felt herself turning red and noticed that the people around them were looking at her sniggering. Rose had never felt so mortified, embarrassed, and all she wanted to do was to go and hide.

Rose couldn't believe she thought he'd done something nice for her, what an idiot she thought, she should have known better about what he thought of her.

They only had sex in the dark and she'd wear a huge, old T-shirt on at night, one that was three times the size she needed. She hated being naked in bed with him and he never tried to take the T-shirt off; she could see the look on his face if he caught her naked, he'd turn his nose up as though he'd been presented a burnt meal in a posh restaurant. He was clearly ashamed of her appearance, and she hadn't felt good enough for him for years.

She'd also discovered he'd mentioned their lack of sex to some friends of theirs, clearly hoping that if she found out, she'd feel pressured in to doing something about it, but she didn't. How could she when she felt about him the way she did? Sex had become robotic and routine. She'd lay back, let him get on with it, then sob in the bathroom afterwards feeling dirty and used.

Not only did she have to worry about her body and how he looks at her in bed, but now she couldn't be comfortable in the clothes he wanted her to wear because she knew if she didn't wear them, she'd have to explain herself, and go through whatever punishment he deemed fit. So, her conclusion was it was best to please him.

Den buying her clothes was him just lining up the next argument for Rose. It's not a gift, it's the beginning of his next act.

* * *

Sleep deprived and unable to think straight, Rose was at breaking point. For the last two weeks, Den had done nothing but push and push and push her, but she wasn't going to let him spoil today. Her friend had recently had a baby, and Rose was going to visit her in hospital. And even though she'd already asked and received his permission to go, Darren had been grumbling all day about having to look after the children while she was out.

It was almost time to leave and Rose went upstairs to get the gift she'd hidden away for her, when Darren called up after her.

'You're really going to go then?' he said softly but slyly.

Rose took a deep breath… she really didn't want another battle with him. He'd been at it all day, making her think it was OK then 'pretending' it wasn't. She knew then she wasn't going but still tried to make the attempt.

'Yes, of course, just like we planned,' she replied without looking at him.

Darren had reached the bedroom now and came over to the wardrobe where she was reaching up for the present.

'I'll miss you; I just want to kiss you and feel your arse.' He was trying to get Rose going by squeezing her bottom… it didn't work, in fact Rose found it more of an insult.

'Well, I'm only going to be out for an hour, so you'll just want me more when I get back.'

'Are the kids fed and watered?'

Rose knew where this was going too – he couldn't look after them without her there and if Rose didn't feed them before she left, they would go hungry. The children had become his latest weapon, to use them and to neglect them.

'Look, can't you see I'm struggling, and I can't concentrate with you doing that?' Rose snapped, as he continued to grope her. Even if they were in a good place in their relationship, she'd have found the way he was touching her degrading and a little out of character.

'Well, if you think you can talk to me like that, then you've got another thing coming. I'm going to my mum's.'

He was pushing her to argue so he had a reason to leave and spoil Rose's plans. He wanted her to beg him; beg him so she could go.

'Who's going to have the kids, then?'

'Well, you, of course, that's a daft question!'

Instead of fighting, Rose thought she'd play him at his own game and take the kids with her, she could ring Helen or Lindsey and see if one of them could watch them for an hour or so. As she pulled herself up on the bed and he grabbed her arm, smiled, and whispered into her ear, 'I'm just joking, you silly cow.'

'OK, well, I need to get going so could you help me get this damn present, I don't know what it's stuck on.'

'Of course, my love,' he said in a tone Rose recognised as a mixture of sarcasm and amusement and he pulled the gift out.

'Typical, eh?' Rose said and heading out of the bedroom.

'When are you giving her the present then?'

Confusion and dread devoured Rose, 'Well, I'm going now, aren't I?'

'You *idiot*! Didn't you hear? I'm going to my mum's.'

Rose wasn't going to give him the satisfaction of winning the game he had started.

'Oh, OK sorry... I'll take the kids with me then.' And she tried to get past him. Darren seemed to try to twist every word, every situation, every piece of body language so that Rose didn't know what he'd said or hadn't said, it was as if he could alter reality and left Rose wondering if what she remembered was in fact what happened.

The world Rose lived in could be altered without her seeing it; like a magician lies in front of everyone's eyes but as a witness, you accept it.

'I think you've lost your keys,' Den said holding them up and swinging them from the end of his finger.

Rose didn't know what came over her, but she completely flipped; she started kicking and hitting the new bed she'd just bought. Darren had got the better of her, she didn't know what was right and what was wrong, what he did and what he didn't do, he'd distort everything she'd say. He was gaslighting her; making her question everything and she was mentally drained.

He looked at Rose in disgust, like she was the vilest thing he'd ever seen as she took out her frustration on the bed.

'Oh my God... you're insane... who would want to be with you... you've completely lost the plot.'

Rose stopped hitting and kicking the bed and spun to look at him, like a hungry wolf been disturbed its meal, she screamed at Darren and fell to the ground and banged her head on the floor. Had she lost the plot? It was like she'd been injected with a craze drug that had taken over her body, and it was Darren who administered it.

As the cheap, rough carpet started making an impression on her forehead, Den's laughter echoed in her head and she glanced up to see the wide grin on his face that shimmered a sense of achievement.

It was always the same, he'd torture Rose for weeks on end and eventually she'd snap, making it look like she was the one who had the problem. She was beside herself this time. He'd got what he wanted again, she wasn't going anywhere.

Rose straggled up using the bed, feeling dizzy and glanced in the mirror, she could see her reflection with the red mark in the middle of her forehead and dark circles under her eyes. Without a care for Darren's reaction and ignoring him, she went to get the kids and left the house.

Rose took the children to the woods and watched them hunting for bears. Guilt had started to set in, they were wonderful children and didn't deserve to live in the madness that was unfolding.

Why couldn't Darren just be normal? I just wanted a normal family life. I had loved him and would have carried on loving him, but I just can't do anything right. I'm a bad wife, a terrible mother, fat, horrible, unwanted, and I'm never going to survive without him.

Rose knew she'd fed his need to control her again, breaking down in front of him like that would have satisfied his need to make her snap for a while and as soon as she stepped back through the door, there would be consequences for her defiance and leaving the house without him.

As Rose expected, the interrogation began as soon as they walked through the door – Where had they been? Who with? Why? Was there a man there? Was she shagging around? No, of course not, no one else would want you!

On and on... Rose spent the afternoon trying to block out his voice, the nasty accusations, and horrible words which were mentally drilling their way into her brain.

At bedtime that night, Rose realised that the children had picked up on the atmosphere; they were typically cheeky, doing anything they could to stay out of bed for as long as possible, apart from on days like this when they would get straight into bed, snuggle down, and look at her like they knew. It broke Rose's heart, she didn't want them to have to change their behaviour like she had to.

* * *

Sat back downstairs, Darren was muttering to himself. Rose could hear some of what he was saying but was trying her hardest to ignore him and zone out but when he said his behaviour was Rose's fault because they hadn't had sex for ages, she was devastated and disgusted all in one. He just loved sticking the knife in, over and over again.

He was relentless.

Darren carried on, 'I mean... we're meant to be married, but that doesn't mean anything these days.' Rose's heart was starting to race. 'All my mates are getting it.'

That was it, Rose couldn't listen to him anymore, she stormed into the kitchen and started to wash the pots. A distraction was needed and keeping busy was therapeutic to

Rose. Darren gave it just the right amount of time before following her – just long enough for Rose to think that she was going to get away with her defiance.

'How dare you walk out when I'm talking to you?'

'Talking *at* me, more like.' Not caring about his reaction, Rose bit back at him.

'Sorry, *what* did you say?' he grunted. 'I didn't quite hear that; do you want to say it to my face?'

Rose was giggling inside, this was so pitiful and felt like they were in the playground at school bickering over the smallest of things. Rose carried on washing-up and ignored him. Then, as she leant over to grab a tea-towel, he gripped Rose's wrist and pulled her towards him, something Rose wasn't expecting.

'Sorry…' he said, taking a long pause, 'what… did… you… say… to me?'

Her heart was racing, and her breathing became erratic, his eyes filled with something akin to mania and Rose was terrified. Pulling her top in his fist he dragged her towards him and screamed in her ear, '*Do I need to ask you again?*'

Rose closed her eyes as he spat at her. Holding her breath, she didn't want him to know she had a shake in her breathing and she looked around the kitchen, anywhere other than his eyes. There was a knife block on the sideboard right beside her, it would be over in minutes and it would be so easy if only she could grab the knife and stab him.

She'd thought about this plenty of times before, the opportunities would present themselves, but she'd never take them. However, if she had to do something in self-defence she'd do it, and this situation felt more concerning than others had. Rose knew it was because she'd tried to stand up for herself for once and he was trying to put her back in her place.

Darren was pressing Rose up against the fridge-freezer, holding her wrists tight by her sides. He could do anything he wanted to, and Rose would powerless against his force and he knew it.

As much as he belittled Rose's body, he still wanted to abuse it – Rose had lost count of the nights she'd wake up to find him having sex with her. There would be a bit of a struggle as she tried to stop him, but he carried on – Rose was his wife and sex was his right, what Rose wanted, or didn't want, was irrelevant.

The way he was breathing, the way he was holding her, the way his eyes flashed made Rose realise this time, there was something different about him. Rose was too scared to reach for the knife in case he got there first so, instead, she kicked him hard in the shin, totally surprising herself and him, then she ran, ran out of the house as fast as she could. Giving them some space would give Rose a chance to work out how to calm the situation down.

But she'd have to return because this is her home and her children depended on her.

* * *

When Rose returned, she was expecting all hell to break loose, but the house was silent and calm. Darren came slowly walking over to her and told her that he wanted them to split up. Freezing from the night air, she let him pass her and didn't respond. He'd done this a million times before and normally she begged him to stay with her, but not tonight. This was what he wanted. He needed Rose to feed his power, and she realised she was letting him.

He tried to goad Rose into another argument, but she wouldn't be taunted. Not even when he told her that she was the one who would be moving out, that he'd be keeping the children, and that she'd be sleeping on the sofa until she found somewhere to live.

Keeping calm as what he said washed over her she tried to understand what he was really saying and what he meant. It was hard at times because she'd had to read between the lines many times before, Den was difficult to read, and it was difficult to know whether he was bluffing.

Rose was numb to his manipulation this time and just walked to the bedroom, grabbed a pillow and duvet and went back downstairs while he followed her around, waiting for that reaction he wanted.

He got none.

Rose couldn't sleep that night and it didn't help that the sofas were cream leather and were cold and slippy. Deciding to check her business messages would be the perfect distraction right now. She'd set up her little business just six months ago – The Perfect Gift Co – the force behind it was in fact, Darren who had got so hot and heavy over her receptionist job that she'd drastically cut her hours down to just four a week.

Den didn't like men talking to her, and she only had a small circle of girlfriends left at work. In the end, it was easier for Rose to quit her job – especially when she'd come up with the idea that she could set up a business from her hobby and could work from home with the business online – surely Darren couldn't argue with that.

Her business idea came after struggling to manage with a baby bag, handbag, and all the things that come with taking a baby out of the house. Rose had made herself a Velcro insert to go into her handbag which held nappies, wipes, and all the essentials. When she'd taken the insert out at baby group, the other mums all wanted one, so she started making them in different colours and patterns on request, and the business grew from there.

After checking and responding to some messages, she finally fell into a fitful sleep.

Weeks later and Rose was still on the sofa, the atmosphere was painful between them but as soon as Darren returned from work it was the kids' bath and then bed time; after that Rose would work on her business.

She'd started to make more money since they'd split up because she spent more time working at it, sometimes she'd stay up until 3.00 a.m. Unable to sleep well on the sofa she'd realised a few hours of solid sleep were better than a night of waking up repeatedly. Over the weeks, Rose had started to gain back her identity. Rekindling friendships online and looking at things she could do that involved the children.

The pressure was off and the time when Darren wasn't there had become stress free and gave Rose time to breathe and the space she mentally needed. The children were enjoying their time, it was almost like Darren had become a lodger as Rose just carried on with things without him, he didn't get too involved with the bedtime routine or meals, so it made things simple.

Rose had become friends with a few local mums in business. Making these friends gave her the courage to have confidence in herself, her decisions, her appearance, and her own identity. It was going to take some time and Rose wasn't in the right place just yet to move forwards but the trickles of compliments, motivations, and encouragement from her new likeminded friends really gave Rose something to look forwards to.

She started to believe she could make the business a success and this could be the answer for her children, she could give them everything they needed. It was her mission to save as much money as possible to be able to move out. It wasn't going to be easy but, for the first time, she had the right thought processes and some support behind her.

One of her new friends, Caroline, had become someone Rose spoke to each day, they had similar interests and their children were of a similar age. They began to meet up at play areas and would talk business strategies, share ideas, and tips. Caroline was a brunette, wore geek style glasses with a leopard rim, and run a caricature business; it was all done with digital software and she worked with other businesses for their branding as well.

Caroline was single and had been for around a year, she'd found her own feet with a new house for her and her children; it was nice for Rose as she was able to confide in her and feel like she wasn't the only one going through what she was. Rose was constantly invited to different events by Caroline and she couldn't refuse, it was just what she needed, the next event was going to be a bit of fun as Caroline had never attended a business speed-networking before and wanted Rose to accompany her.

CHAPTER SEVEN

The day had come for Rose and Caroline to attend this new speed-networking for businesses, they had sixty seconds to talk about their business and how they could help the other business owners they meet. It seemed rather formal, and both had dressed for the occasion, in their smart clothes and high heels, they were sat next to each other and surrounded by others in a square waiting for the bell to ring.

They were giggling like school girls at a school disco, it was more nerves than anything else, they didn't know what to expect. The other people around them were mixed with formal and more informal clothing, they weren't overdressed but they were causing some attention. Lip gloss on, blusher on, mascara on, Rose hadn't put as much effort into her appearance as she had today for a long time and she felt confident.

Business cards at the ready and they were about to go, there was a line at one side waiting to enter to follow the queue down and sit at their first allocated seats. Rose and Caroline had a card with names on and a tick box they had to answer – would like to do business with –

YES/NO/MAYBE. The announcer was a successful business woman in the area, someone a lot of people, including Rose and Caroline, looked up to, officially opened the event. Everyone took their first seats and once the bell rang, that was it – sixty seconds.

Ding the bell sounded and there was a roar of chatter among the business people trying to get in every second. Rose was sat opposite a gentleman in his forties who had a signage business which would be perfect if she had a shop, Rose could begin to dream about what her future might hold, she looked over at Caroline who was faced with a lady in her late thirties; they were busily chatting away as well.

Ding – sixty seconds went fast, now they had to swap, and Rose had to talk about her business to Greg who was ready and waiting. Rose was a bit out of practice and felt a bit silly as she handmade things, she felt a little out of place, but as she spoke, Greg mentioned that he had someone he knew who owned a baby shop and could connect them about stocking her range.

The potential from this was something Rose didn't expect, she soon realised that everyone could be a customer because she learnt that you don't know who someone else knows and that's what networking was about.

Ding – time to switch seats, Rose stayed where she was, and Greg moved on, Rose quickly put a tick next to YES for Greg and felt excited to meet the next business owner.

A manic half an hour of networking and it was time for a break, Rose and Caroline nipped to the ladies' room to powder their noses and quickly swap notes. They were both giggling, were getting excited, oohed and aahed at what the other said.

After they'd reapplied their lip gloss, they went back to their seats for the next half. The second half went faster than the first, Rose felt like she needed a glass of wine to deal with the amount of people she'd met in a short space of time.

Afterwards, Rose urged Caroline to stay and have a drink with her, she needed to talk to her about someone she'd met.

Tim, a highly successful business man in marketing, he had black hair and wore a tailor-made suit and he'd grabbed Rose's attention. They had hit it off straight away, and it felt like they were speed-dating rather than speed-networking.

Tim had complimented Rose on the achievements she'd made in such a short time and Rose was so bashful, not used to such compliments. There was clearly chemistry between them, but Rose was out of practice and didn't know how to respond properly. Tim was such a gentleman and had offered to help – he told her if there was anything he could do to help, she just had to let him know. Rose could think of a lot of marketing questions to ask.

Tim and Rose had instantly clicked and from then on, they were emailing each other, then Facebook messaging, then texting.

* * *

Rose and Darren had been separated for a couple of months but were still living together as neither of them could afford to move out. At first, things were OK, and Rose could handle the tension, but it soon became a living hell. She never knew when he'd be there and would sometimes just feel him watching her like she was under surveillance, it felt intimidating and scary.

Darren had started to wake Rose up in the middle of the night in the attempt to sort things out. A week ago, Darren had offered to switch and sleep on the sofa and, she took the opportunity of having the bed for a bit because she was starting to ache from the position she had to lay each night on the sofa.

Sleeping back in the bed without Darren, Rose felt comfortable and was able to snuggle into the covers, she'd put fresh bedding on and enjoyed a bath before bed to relax a little more. But it didn't take long for something to change. Darren started to wake Rose up again trying to get things sorted.

Rose was reminded of the early days of their relationship and was confused and wanted a break. He couldn't believe she was happy with the way things were going or that she was pleased that she'd regained a little of her life back. Rose was getting comfortable with her prospects and he didn't like it one bit.

One morning, Rose woke up with Darren next to her. He'd started climbing into bed while Rose was asleep which completely freaked her out. She didn't want to risk anything else happening so went quickly back to sleeping on the sofa where she felt more comfortable.

The lack of sleep started to make her ill and the stress of the situation was getting to her, Rose confided in Caroline, but she had her own problems to deal with.

Soon, Tim became someone Rose could speak to, they had plenty of business chats over the weeks and they'd met up to discuss her marketing plan for her business. This particular night, their conversation turned more personal than business – it wasn't anything harmful just not fully business related, and Tim managed to take her mind off everything going on without knowing what he was doing.

Darren had become more intimidating and was picking arguments with everyone. The pressure on Rose was sky-high, and she'd become numb once again to what he was saying to her.

'You're useless, you'll regret this for the rest of your life, no one would have you because you're a nut case. I'll tell the courts you have bipolar, you're a slut, you're a bad mum, the kids would be better off without you. I'll tell them you've had three different counsellors.'

The threats went on and on, Rose tried to shut the door to her emotions one by one.

* * *

His threatening stare and constant demands weren't working and Rose soon realised she'd started to win. Rose was able to confide in Tim one day when they'd been following up on Rose's marketing plan and how she was going to implement it. She broke down in tears and thanked Tim for his help, he didn't have to help her.

For the first time she cried on his shoulder, she couldn't give him the whole story, she barely knew him, but he'd become suspicious of her situation and knew all wasn't as it seemed. Tim, for now, listened to Rose, he recognised that's what she needed. It gave Rose time to recharge and prepare for another day filled with her favourite blank expression for Darren.

This particular day, Darren cornered Rose and said, 'I want £200 by next week or I'll be throwing you out.' He was trying higher tactics to get Rose to crumble, she didn't respond, and he left her alone for the rest of the day. Later that day, Rose told Tim what had been said, he tried to reassure her that Darren must be bluffing, no one was that mean and do such a thing.

She wanted to believe Tim, but she had a big feeling that he was wrong, Tim was thinking logically but Darren was everything but logic. Rose was glad she was able to tell someone what was going on, she didn't want any advice or to second guess Darren's words but just for someone to listen and Tim had become that person. It was like a relief.

Although they'd met through business, they'd become more than connections, they'd become friends. Caroline had continued to see Rose but had some big business meetings to attend that were going to sky rocket her business, Rose spent the time with her getting excited and celebrating, the kids enjoying each other's company.

They spoke about Tim and Caroline suggested Rose let her hair down a bit, Rose took it on the chin because she didn't know what was going on behind closed doors, the seriousness of everything, Rose couldn't do anything to complicate the situation.

However, Rose was able to giggle with her about how cute they both thought he was, and that he was worth going into business with just to enjoy his company, it was fun to imagine the scenarios that Caroline would come up with.

The week passed, and Darren kept to his word and re-warned Rose, 'Tomorrow, if you don't have the £200 for me, you're out.'

Was he bluffing like Tim had said?

Rose remained silent, she wasn't going to agitate it further, but Darren came in with something that told her he was going to go through with his threat.

'Believe you me, Rose... I can be a right nasty bastard – even more so than I've ever been before! Do you understand that?'

Rose smiled back at him, trying to hide her true anxiety of what was about to happen. Rose had always wondered if Darren knew what he was doing to her and she'd strived to get through it thinking he hadn't a clue. This moment ticked a box in her head.

* * *

Before 'moving out day' arrived, Darren had a day off work and decided they were going to spend it as a family. Rose had no choice but to go along with it, he'd threatened if she didn't spend time as a family then she'd be thrown out there and then. Rose was still in two minds whether he'd go through with kicking her out, but he was convincing that it was going to happen.

It was an uncomfortable day. He'd insisted on taking the children to the local play area and Rose knew she'd have to sit next to him and have a coffee as they 'talked'. Darren spent most of the time questioning her and telling her what he thought of her, Rose was on her best behaviour and held her tongue, there was so much she wanted to say to defend herself. Darren was wrong about most of what he was saying, he only had a bunch of assumptions.

The kids were having a wonderful time, and fighting back the tears Rose, wondered whether it would be easier to take responsibility for everything and go back to the way things were. The thought of not seeing her children and them being unhappy was too much for her to bear.

Lunch was spent at a restaurant and Darren played happy families as though nothing had happened to bring them to this point.

It was painful for Rose to pretend everything was OK and Darren's behaviour was unsettling and concerning. Something was seriously wrong.

When Darren let her go to the bathroom, she sent a text to both Caroline and Tim.

Hi, I'm going to pop my location on just in case, something doesn't feel right about Darren, I'm OK for now and I'll message you when I can. If there's something wrong,

I'll prank call you. I feel better if I do this because then I know I have a backup plan but please don't worry for now.

Rose sent the message, re-read it and saw it looked confusing, but she didn't know what else to do; she couldn't put her finger on why Darren's behaviour was so disturbing.

As she walked back to the table, putting a slight smile on her face and asking how everyone was getting on with their lunch, Den sensed something was up. Rose tried to keep everything 'normal', she played the part a little but not too much. Millie-Rose was enjoying tucking into her sponge pudding dessert and Harrison wanted to sit on his mummy's lap for a hug. Everything seemed calm.

The afternoon was spent at a playground adventure park, another play area for the kids to get involved with. Rose enjoyed it when she could focus on just Millie-Rose and Harrison. There was a little petting area with chickens, rabbits, and sheep; there were lots of excited screams from the children as they petted the different animals and watched them doing their everyday pecking, hopping, and bleating.

It was a mild day, and the weather was nice, and an outsider looking in they appeared to be the perfect family. No one could tell what was going on behind closed doors.

Later, the children, all tuckered out from all the fun and their tummies full, they went straight to bed. Rose wished them goodnight, placed a kiss on their foreheads, and rolled off the goodnight wish she did each night, 'Goodnight, don't let the bedbugs bite and don't let nibble at your toes either.'

Millie-Rose always giggled when Rose popped their toes in her mouth as she pretended to nibble them and say they were tasty.

Rose made her way downstairs and was ready for a cup of tea. Walking into the kitchen, she found Darren cooking something on the stove.

'Oh, sorry I'll get out your way.' Rose turned on the spot and was about to leave. 'I'm making some for you as well.' Darren stopped her in her tracks.

'I'm not hungry, I was going to grab a cup of tea and get on with some work, thank you though.'

'Rose, look...' Darren paused, and Rose turned around trying not to be concerned. 'I want to make it up to you, I know you're not going to do it first this time, so I thought I would.'

Confusion furrowed her brow.

'But you were going to throw me out? You have broken up with me.'

His smile sent chills down her spine. 'Things are always said in the heat of the moment, aren't they?'

'This hasn't been the heat of the moment though, Den, this has been upsetting and very serious to me, don't you realise how you've made me feel? How scared I've been?'

'Oh, I'm so sorry if I gave you that impression,' he replied a sinister edge to his voice that chilled her further.

Rose was even more confused and didn't know what to do, she'd already decided she couldn't live like this, she couldn't deal with the stress, the lack of sleep, the upset.

At first, there was something wrong every few months, then it crept weekly, then daily, and now it could be minutes between his episodes. Rose couldn't tell whether she was coming or going. She never knew what Darren really wanted.

Her eyes filled with tears. 'I'm sorry, Darren but this isn't fair.'

'What's not fair? I've cooked tea, I've apologised, I've spent the whole day out with you all, and paid for it, what more do you want?'

Anxiety was coursing through her veins as Darren started slowly walking towards her.

'Don't you want our family back together? Don't you want a home? Don't you want to see those children that love you so dearly?' He began circling her as if he was assessing his prey. He didn't stop.

'You know you can't leave, don't you? You know that if you do, you will never see those children ever again. You know you have no way out of this, don't you?'

The tears started to spill down her cheeks. Darren was waiting for her to reply as she started to step back from him, trying to get out of his way and stop him circling her.

'I think we've had a long day and we both need to just go to bed,' Rose urged and gave it a try.

Darren caught the back of her foot, tripping her up, she fell onto her bottom with her head hitting the wall. Darren sniggered, and a frenzied sneer took over his face. Rose held the back of her head as the dull ache had started to seep through, there was no blood, but a bump was developing, her bottom was sore, and she couldn't move for a moment.

'I wouldn't want you if someone paid me to have you.' He enjoyed every word he spoke down to her as she was cradling her head. 'I think you need to be taught a lesson, one you will never forget.' He turned his back on Rose and went towards the kitchen counter, Rose looked up and could see the knife block there.

She wasn't going to risk it, the adrenaline rushed through her body in fear of what he was going to do, she turned over and stumbled up using the radiator as her aid.

'Where are you going?' Den raised his voice as she got to the front door and struggled to get the keys to turn. Rose looked back, she couldn't see anything in his hand, but he was coming towards her, as the door opened she ran, ran as fast as she could. She didn't know what he was going to do, but she needed to get out of there.

There was no going back now.

CHAPTER EIGHT

Tears coursed down Rose's face; she was shivering, and her breath was fogging in front of her every time she sobbed. She looked at the time on her phone, half an hour had passed. Her eyes glazed over as she looked around. There was no one around, no cars in sight. She'd given Tim a missed call like they'd planned when she left the house. She'd got around the corner certain that Darren wasn't behind and stopped long enough to message Tim about what had happened.

She couldn't ring him, she was out of breath and in tears. Sat in a slushy, muddy puddle Rose didn't move; she wouldn't care if she was cemented there like a statue. Shaking her head in her hands; tears broke through her fingers and she bellowed as she felt a pain, her heart aching, her stomach churning, and the flood of sickness overcame her. Her head was still sore.

She thought about Millie-Rose and Harrison, they were oblivious to what was going on around them. Rose had faith that he wouldn't hurt them, she felt he'd only ever done something to prove a point. They were asleep now and Rose guessed she was being slagged off to his family. Rose would be there in the morning for when they woke up.

Then, creeping around the corner she saw a car appear and mount the kerb near her.

Her eyes were blurry and sore; she looked up at the car and saw a man getting out of a dark blue car. Rose tried to focus her eyes, but everything looked fuzzy and before she could see him clearly, she heard a deep voice, 'What are you doing out here on your own?'

She stood up feeling dizzy and almost drunk as Tim took her in his arms and held her.

Never one to ask for help, Rose didn't know what to say. He'd offered her help with the business and now what she was asking was personal and she had no idea what his reaction would be. She had no idea how he'd become captivated by her sense of humour, her intelligence, and her big brown eyes.

Holding Rose in his arms he said, 'You're shivering and ice-cold.'

He took off his jacket and placed it around her shoulders then slowly guided her to his car. She was shocked at how his arms instantly made her feel safe and that she was allowing him to guide her and care for her. She wasn't used to this gentleness from a man. Tim ran around the car, got in, and turned the heat up high.

'Let's get you to my place and we can try to sort this out.'

When they arrived at his house, Tim opened the passenger's door and helped Rose out of the car, clicked his key fob to lock it and then continued to assist Rose, felt her tremble as her wet clothes and hair were hit with the frosty air. Tim opened the front door which led straight into the living room and Rose saw that there was a log file roaring with heat. She ran towards it and collapsed in a heap in front of it. She could feel the flickers of the flames against her skin.

Tim went to collect some blankets and a dressing gown to snuggle her up in; he then continued to the kitchen where he put the kettle on. Once settled with a hot cup of tea, Rose began to tell him what had happened but soon found herself sobbing again. Tim held her in his arms. He was so warm, and Rose's tears were welcome on his shoulder, although he wished they weren't there he knew they were needed. He stroked her hair and cradled her in his strong arms as the firelight glistened.

Rose couldn't bear it, questions kept filling her head. Why did she think this was normal for couples? Why couldn't she have left sooner? Why didn't she read the stupid leaflet? Why couldn't she see the signs? Why didn't anyone shake her, so she'd see Darren's true colours? Would she have taken notice if they had?

She could see in Tim's eyes that he didn't understand why she was with Darren. How could she even start to explain to a man like him?

She'd never been with someone who would bring her warm towels when she was wet. She'd never known a man leave his house in the middle of a stormy night to pick up an almost stranger. Although they had spent hours talking over the last few months, they'd only met in person a handful of times. Was she right to be here? What did he want from her? What did she have to give a man like Tim?

She explained to Tim that the children were the reason she was still in this situation. Darren had threatened her and used Millie-Rose and Harrison as weapons so often that it was safer for her to stay with him. Countless times he'd said he'd get custody of the children and tell the court how Rose had severe bipolar disorder – which wasn't true. Rose was so scared of losing them that she'd been to the doctor to check if she did have the disorder. After all the torment over the years, she has started to believe him, but her doctor assured her she was fine.

'Thank you so much, you don't know how much it means,' she began, hugging her cup with her hands.

Tim sat on his cream, leather sofa near Rose and cautiously asked, 'Where are your family? Do they know what's going on?'

'They're in Liverpool. I moved to York for university, met Darren and ended up staying here. I've always wanted to go back. Anyway, I don't speak to them that much and I haven't been back for over two years now.'

Rose's face washed with desperation and Tim thought it was best to change the tone and lighten things up.

'OK, come on... tell me what's your favourite food?'

Rose smiled and replied, 'Mexican.'

'How about I take you out for Mexican on Saturday night?' Tim casually asked.

'You already know my answer,' Rose spoke with a huge grin and a giddy feeling came over her; she didn't care how she was going to sort it with Darren, but she was going to go and enjoy herself.

A couple of hours had gone by and it was past midnight when Tim asked a nervous question, 'So... what do you want to do from here? Shall I take you home now?' Rose knew she couldn't stay with him forever and had to be back for the children for the morning.

'I need to go back to my kids and be with them when they wake up.'

'If I'm honest, Rose, I don't want to take you back there, but I understand why you have to go. I'll take you if you promise me you'll get in touch straight away if you need me, it doesn't matter what time it is, it doesn't matter what day it is, or where you are; I *will* come and get you *and* the children. I promise you that I will be there no matter what.'

Tim was looking Rose in the eyes and wanted her to believe him, wanted her to feel secure, and know she had a safe place to go.

He didn't know that she'd already started to realise she was able to confide in him and was relieved that she had someone to listen to her.

'Come on then, I'll get my keys.' Tim held her hand all the way to the car, giving affection that made her feel warm.

The roads were clear as they made their way to her house, so he dropped her off at the end of the street to avoid Den hearing the car pulling up.

'Thank you, Tim, I don't know what to say.'

'You don't have to say anything; just promise me you will let me know if you need me and that you won't hesitate to get in touch if you need me?'

'I promise.' Rose smiled the first genuine smile she'd given anyone other than her children for a long time and opened the car door when Tim said, 'Rose.'

She looked back and Tim took hold of her hand, looked deep into her eyes, and kissed her fingers as he whispered, 'Goodnight, Rose.'

CHAPTER NINE

The sun filtered through a small gap in the beige curtains onto Rose's face the next morning. She woke with a wince and a smile; she was thinking about last night and how Tim made her feel.

Rose rolled over and let out a scream. 'Ahhhhh, what the actual f… do you think you're doing?' Darren was staring back at her like he'd been watching her all night. Rose was initially terrified he'd seen her with Tim, but if that had been the case, he wouldn't have waited until the morning to ask her where she'd been.

'It's my bed too you know, I can't sleep on the sofa any longer.' And he blew his cigarette smoke into her face. Rose was already irritated and out of patience with him.

'I've told you to set up a single bed in the dining room or something, you can't just do this!'

'Well, I have and now I'm going to get ready for work,' Darren said with the attitude of a teenager.

When Darren had finally gone to work, and Rose had got the children up, she brewed up a hot mug of tea. This was Rose's morning routine and another fifteen cups of tea would follow before the day was out. Millie-Rose was playing with her kitchen and making Rose and Harrison cups of tea with her toy tea bags and miniature cups. Harrison was playing with his walker that resembled a car and was making his way over to Millie-Rose to bash into her feet which he loved to do.

Rose sat down and snuggled into her warm, leather sofa and hugged her mug of tea. She watched her two children with a smile on her face and couldn't imagine life without them. She'd wanted to be a mum since she was ten years old; it was a huge life aspiration for her and she always wanted to get it 'right' and be the best she could be.

Millie-Rose handed Rose a pretend cup of tea and smiled. She was happy and gave Rose a long-lasting hug. They had a true mummy and daughter unbreakable bond and Rose valued this as she felt it was missing from her adult relationships. Harrison bashed his way through his toys and joined in by hugging Rose's leg as he couldn't quite reach over his car walker. They all said loudly together, 'awww' and giggled.

Rose was overcome with emotion and her eyes were filling with tears. She couldn't conceal them; she knew her children would have a better life if she and Darren finally lived apart. Even though they'd officially split up three months ago, they were still sharing a house and Darren had become increasingly more impatient and angrier with them all since then.

Rose's parents had divorced when she was a child and she'd always been adamant her children wouldn't go through that, but she was starting to realise that staying with Darren was doing them more damage than good.

She'd often daydreamed about having the perfect family, beautiful house, white picket fence, the works. But it was becoming clearer that wasn't her future if she stayed where she was, and as much as she didn't want her children to see how ugly divorce could get, it was looking more and more likely that that's where they were headed.

Rose's dreams had changed a lot recently; she now imagined herself homeless, poor, and struggling for the rest of her life. She was afraid her children would follow the pattern of Darren's family's lifestyle: drug abuse, violence, and involvement with the police. Rose could see her life was spiralling out of control and that the mould was starting to set in. Her business was starting to grow, and she was proud of what she'd achieved in such a short amount of time.

Darren thought she'd fail and made sure Rose was fully aware of this, but she believed in filling her life with positive people who helped you and encouraged you. This would keep her fighting for a better life. Rose had begun to focus her mind, and she managed to start having little positive moments that were like water dropping into a still lake. Although small at first, they rippled out through her and her confidence started to grow.

Rose kept telling herself what she'd learnt through research, *it takes three years to start making a profit on a business and to begin to pay yourself.* She started talking positively to herself in the mirror – which was difficult to begin with. This was going to be her nest-egg, and she was going to see it through; she wanted her children to see how hard-working she was and to be able to provide for them.

She wanted to move out of the estate she lived in, even though others told her there was nothing wrong with this and her auntie Lucy had told her, 'It doesn't matter where your house is as long as you make it a home. If you can step in through the front door and feel that homeliness, then that's all that matters.'

Rose held onto this and made the house feel warm and with her own stamp on it on the inside, but it still wasn't enough and didn't take away from the fact that the area didn't feel right for the children.

There were often disturbances down the street and Rose didn't like Millie-Rose and Harrison going out in the back garden in the summer. The neighbour's mum would be swearing at her children and every other word would be inappropriate. Darren had never seemed to mind because his family lived on the same street and it was like he was immune to the language and foul behaviour.

Millie-Rose had started making play dinner for them all now; Rose loved to feed their imaginations and play along. How easy life seemed for children. Sugar-coating it or cotton-wooling life's everyday problems and concerns in children's lives was something that frustrated Rose, she sometimes wished she could go back to being a carefree child and worry about not having the correct coloured pen for a project. No one prepares you for the reality of what life really is as you grow into adulthood.

Rose often tried to enter the carefree bubble with them, the most important thing to Millie-Rose and Harrison was to make plastic sweetcorn in a pan and pretend it was warm and yummy. They would giggle uncontrollably when Rose nibbled her plastic food.

Rose would do anything for her children and they were just one of what felt like a thousand reasons to stay and suffer in this situation. There seemed to be only one hundred reasons to leave.

Included in the hundred reasons to leave were her health and sanity, to see her family more and regain friendships, to be independent, and not feel like she was suffocated. But these were over-shadowed by the thousand reasons to stay she'd convinced herself of. She'd be homeless with her children, there would be no money, and she was already in debt. Darren and his family would come after her, she'd have to leave all her possessions, and it might mean closing the business she'd started to build.

Fears of making the wrong choice for her children, fears that she couldn't cope, were all niggling at her conscious. Rose had baggage and would be alone; Rose wasn't worth the trouble. Most of the reasons had been drummed into her by Darren, and he'd tied her up in knots financially.

There were too many consequences if she left so staying seemed like the safest option especially as she'd become immune to Darren's ways. It was only recently that she'd started to feel what happiness was like and the urge to change the way her life was going. Could she truly break free? Rose was still worrying about the night before and Darren's behaviour, she felt it could only get worse.

* * *

Rose felt exhausted by the evening, thinking through the options she had, which would be best for her children, and the dilemma of how she was going to achieve it. But, the more she thought about it, the more reasons she found that prevented her from escaping.

Darren was at work and this gave Rose some time alone as the kids were tucked up in bed. She decided to text Tim, *Hi, how are you? I've been playing kitchen with the kids and having a break for the day. Thank you for last night.* Rose made herself a hot steaming mug of tea. Hugging the mug, she awaited Tim's reply.

Tim didn't take long to get back to her, he always had his phone close to him for his business. You don't have to thank me, glad you had a break. You must be exhausted. If you're free, can I call you after 7.30 p.m.?

Rose blushed, and a huge smile spread across her face; it felt good that someone cared for her and knew what was going on. There was no way she could confide in her family anymore as Darren knew if she'd spoken to them. They would give him the cold shoulder even if they didn't mean to. Rose was beginning to feel there was light at the end of the tunnel even if it was so far in the distance she couldn't quite see it clearly yet. It was all thanks to Tim treating her like a human; something so simple could change her mood.

She decided to do some business emailing while waiting for her call from Tim. Rose loved her little business which she'd set up through her own hobbies and ideas. She was naturally good at art, just like her parents, and she was super-creative. Her business, The Perfect Gift Co., provided a unique gift service; from a box of chocolates to a bunch of flowers.

Her gifts were all handmade, and she found it therapeutic – it gave her mind a focus. The business was also a great escape from Darren; she'd work in the dining room while he was in the living room watching the TV on an evening. *Why didn't I think of this sooner?* she often thought. The peace and quiet she got while working, talking to customers, and making friends had changed so much in her.

Rose set up the home business when Darren made working at a 'normal' job impossible. After every shift there would be a problem and he would interrogate her; it could be as simple as she'd reapplied make-up or had given someone a lift home from work. The business was an escape for her; she'd even managed to make some new friends with other mums who ran their own businesses. These new connections started to build her confidence, and she started to feel wanted and valued by others and her emotions were starting to reappear.

Rose had become used to not responding to different situations and would let comments from Darren wash over her head. She was becoming less like a robot and feeling more human-like. Rose found it easier to live like a robot, but her identity was slipping, and she'd become more than just isolated.

She'd lost some weight over the last couple of months and her business connections had started to compliment her. This feeling of success was a rare for Rose. It had also given her the confidence to realise that she didn't deserve what had been happening to her, and she was regaining her self-worth.

Rose's phone rang, and Tim's name flashed up. Rose jumped to her phone but let it ring a couple of times and then answered, 'Oh, hi, sorry, I was just emailing a few customers.' She thought that would impress him.

'Hi, sorry I couldn't speak earlier, I was just finishing up in a meeting. I guess we're both busy with work, eh?' Tim laughed along with Rose. Rose hadn't any idea on how to lead a conversation with someone she was falling for, it had been so long since she had to flirt.

'I've been thinking about last night,' Rose said nervously as she chewed her lip.

Tim, gentleman-like as he was, replied, 'I meant what I said, I'm here for you no matter what.' They spoke for a few minutes, Rose was in a bubble and wasn't thinking about anything else when Darren barged in and took the phone off her.

'Who's this?' Tim had clearly hung up. Darren had appeared out of nowhere, she hadn't heard him sneak into the house.

Darren looked at her and demanded, 'Who was it?' His

glare pierced her skin for a moment before he grabbed her wrist and repeated himself and shouted in her face. She closed her eyes, wishing he wouldn't spray her with his spit. Rose felt that she should try to stand up for herself for once and not to be afraid. *What's the worst he could do?* she thought to herself.

'He's just a friend who's been helping me, actually, and, we separated a few months ago so it doesn't matter who I talk to.'

Darren threw her wrist back at her. 'You disgust me! You haven't even left this house. What do I tell the kids when they wake up to a different man in the house every morning?' Rose didn't even answer, there was no point, he wouldn't listen to her.

Rose had never slept with anyone behind Darren's back, but he constantly accused her of cheating on him. Darren was overly paranoid, jealous, and had once said that Millie-Rose could have been another man's child and made her sound like a slut who had slept with a hundred men in the last week.

Rose lacked self-confidence and hated herself naked; she used to sleep with Darren with her pyjama top on because he made her feel like her small breasts were non-existent and her baby belly made her the largest woman in the world. Darren's views of Rose became hers and it didn't take long before Rose couldn't look in the mirror without believing every negative word Darren had ever said about her.

Darren had stormed off in a huff shouting random insults, but all Rose could think and worry about was the children waking up and hearing everything that was going on.

There was a sound coming from Rose's computer desk and she saw it was her business mobile ringing. She looked down and saw that her personal one was smashed. Tim was calling her; she quickly ran over and answered it, so it wouldn't ring anymore and hoped Darren hadn't heard it. *Thank God there was another phone nearby*, Rose thought.

Tim spoke, 'Are you OK? I'm on my way, so don't worry.'

Rose quickly squeezed out a few words, 'Stay on the phone.' She placed it in her pocket and kept it connected to Tim. She felt a little safer knowing that someone was on the end of the phone listening in.

Darren came barging back in with her pink holdall stuffed with some of her clothes. 'You can leave now – anything you don't take now, you won't get back.'

Rose was in shock but held back her tears; she was going to be strong. 'NO, I'm not going, this is my home too. You have family nearby and mine are miles away so maybe you should go and then we can sort out the rest when the children aren't around.'

Rose couldn't believe she'd put her foot down and stuck up for herself for once, but as soon as she felt pride in her new-found confidence, Darren knocked it out of her. Clearly it was a weak attempt.

'You left me, and you moved out for a few nights a couple of weeks ago so why don't you just go back to your mum's?'

Darren turned his back on Rose, he went to the front door, and threw her bag out onto the front yard as if to say, *I'm the boss*. Darren had left her before and he didn't seem to have a problem with it, so Rose couldn't understand why he was being like this.

Rose wished she'd had the locks changed when she had the chance those two weeks ago. The police and housing association weren't helpful. Tim had suggested she contact them and inform them of what was going on; both had responded with, 'I'm sorry but it's his home too and he has a right to stay there so, if you get the locks changed, we would have to allow entry.'

Somehow that didn't seem fair, especially when she'd explained what he was doing to her and that she had two children under the age of five in the house. The police told her she could report him, and they would make a note on the system but because he hadn't done anything criminal, it was unlikely to go further, at the worst-case scenario the police would hold him but after four hours he would still be released and able to return home, back to Rose and the children.

CHAPTER TEN

Rose had started to lose faith in her finding a service or someone with a title able to help. She'd never felt so alone and afraid for the safety of the children and herself so much before.

Rose hadn't done anything about this before because Darren had not only threatened, humiliated, bullied, intimidated, emotionally abused, harassed, and manipulated her, but he had debt of £6,000 hanging over her shoulders. The debt was all in Rose's name and had built up because Darren had been black listed on getting any loans or store cards out, Rose had furnished the house, paid for shopping and unpaid bills with her ability to have credit.

How was she meant to get out of this on her own?

Rose often thought suicide was her only escape but even that wasn't the answer as she couldn't bear the thought of what might happen to her children; they were keeping her alive. Darren was clearly a very clever man to be able to make someone feel like this and although uneducated, he wasn't stupid; he'd manipulated Rose so well that she'd believed her behaviours were causing the problems in their marriage, she'd gone to the extent of seeing counsellor after counsellor about it.

Rose went outside and realised her pink holdall wasn't alone on the lawn; Darren's dad, three sisters, and two brothers had joined it. Rose's heart started to thump out of her chest; what was this? Assistance? What were they going to do?

Rose remembered why she feared Darren and all those reasons why she kept her mouth shut and had started to doubt her decision to separate from him. Darren wasn't alone, and his family would back him up when he needed it, they were a family not to get on the wrong side of.

The stories Rose heard Darren talking about over the years of his family's achievements with crime and their attitude towards those they don't like. Rose not only feared Darren, but she feared what he was a part of. Rose began to think this was more difficult than she originally thought it was going to be.

Rose knew what they were capable of; his dad had just been released from prison for assaulting a police officer; the year before, Darren's brother had been questioned on suspicion of attempted murder, and all his sisters had ASBOs.

Nevertheless, his family appeared in this moment to be intimidating Rose with their unavoidable glare and their folded armed stance. Rose never thought that Darren would get his family involved as he'd always tried to keep his life as separate as could, that was until Rose and Darren had moved closer to them with no choice due to finances.

Rose's hands were starting to sweat with nerves as she looked at them all but was unable to look in their eyes as they were still glaring at her, their eyes fixated on her every move. Crazy thoughts were spinning around her head; were they going to beat her up? Drag her down the street? Go into the house and smash up the rest of her things?

She thought about her precious children inside sleeping, oblivious, thankfully, to what was going on. A sharp stab went through her body and hit her heart. What would happen to them? Would she even be allowed to see them?

Rose was trying her hardest not to show the fear she felt inside. Anger was overcoming her, and she thought about all she'd done for Darren's family. She'd been nothing but polite and helpful. She'd helped create CVs so a couple of them could apply for jobs, babysitting, and even considered fostering his sister's children when they were going to be taken away. She realised none of what she'd done for them would mean anything; they were unappreciative and anyway, blood was thicker than water.

Within no time, Tim's car came speeding around the corner and pulled up outside the house. Tim got out and asked, 'Is everything OK, Rose?' She couldn't speak. She was in a fog of her thoughts and fears, but then made her way to Tim staggering as if she was drunk.

Darren shouted over, 'The boyfriend come to help, has he? Like I said, get what you want now because whatever you leave, is left.' And he laughed.

Rose could see all her fears coming true and as she realised what was happening, she was glad that Tim was there with her.

Darren's family stood in a line in front of the house like an army's front-line defence. Tim couldn't believe what he was seeing and even though Rose had told him lots of what had gone on, it's hard to believe until you see it.

Tim couldn't believe anyone could treat another human like this or how Rose had ended up in this situation; he believed she deserved much better. Putting his hand on her shoulder, he whispered, 'I'll help, don't worry, you can stay with me.'

They were outnumbered, and Rose had no choice but to leave. She couldn't stand the thought of her children seeing anymore incidents involving Darren's abuse. Millie-Rose had seen him throw things at her, seen him screaming and shouting in her face, she'd even watched as he'd stood over Rose while she cleaned and told her how rubbish and useless she was at it.

There were times when he'd locked them in the house and Millie-Rose didn't understand why she couldn't play in the garden. Her sweet, clever daughter had already learnt the art of being seen and not heard, and was slowly teaching these skills to Harrison, who she protected like a lioness with her cubs.

All this was scaring them and clearly, if Darren wasn't leaving and judging by the fact her belongings were strewn across the garden and her path was blocked by his family, and she had no one but Tim to help her, she had no choice.

Rose had a plan, she'd return once it was all was calm and quiet; she didn't know how, but she knew this wasn't the end and her children would be with her soon.

Her heart was breaking but at that moment in time, this was the right thing to do, it had to be.

Rose walked up to the house and went inside, trying to keep her head held high. Tim was behind her, but Darren put out his arm and said, 'Sorry, mate, I don't allow strangers into my home.'

Rose looked back at Tim and asked, 'Can you put the things the yard in the car?' as calmly as she could. Tim nodded back and quietly began to load her belongings into the boot taking care to ignore the watching family.

Twenty minutes of rushing around gathering her things

together while listening to Darren's immature, chav-like sister, Katie, mouthing some of the vilest things Rose had ever heard, were starting to take their toll.

'What are the kids meant to think? Mummy walked out on them? Is that who you've been shagging out there? I can see where that's gonna go,' she said, laughing in Rose's face. 'You're scum. The kids are better off without you.'

Rose tried to ignore these childish comments, but they cut deep; she wasn't leaving her children, she was being forced out. Rose knew what Katie was saying wasn't true and resisted the urge to retaliate. She held back the tears stinging her eyes, and answered back in her head, what do you know – you live in a gutter. My children don't need an auntie like you: thief, druggy, scum.

Darren was lording about and laughing at the things Katie was saying. His behaviour finally made Rose realise that she hadn't imagined it all these years, he really was vile. Rose just wanted to go into her children's bedrooms and take her precious children out of their beds and with her, they are meant to be with me Rose thought.

Rose had never felt so desperate in her whole life, she didn't want to have to be forced out and leave them, but she knew it wouldn't be the end and she won't ever stop fighting for her children, she just needed to be clever about it.

Tim was hurt to see Rose in this mess; no one should have to go through this. He loaded the last of her things, glad that things with their audience had been quiet.

It was a mild evening, but it was starting to spit rain as Rose walked out of the house one last time. Just as she was about to get into the car, Darren said, 'I'll need the key too.'

Rose wasn't going to give them back – it was still her house too, and it was her last link to being able to get her children back.

'While my name is on the house, I will have a key and only when it's removed I'll hand over the key.'

She could get the house for all anyone knew.

'I need those keys now. How do I know you're not gonna come in when I'm out?' Darren said coolly, and before they knew it, one of Darren's brothers, John, was running towards them. Rose got in the car, but he pulled the door open. Tim turned the key and revved the engine, so he could drive off quickly.

What happened next was beyond comprehension.

Tim started to drive off with John still hanging on to the open passenger door and with the adrenaline pumping, the car was spluttering forwards slowly. He was terrified he'd cause John a serious injury.

John pulled Rose so hard that she was dragged out of the car and flung to the moving ground beneath her. Slamming on the brakes, Tim jumped out of the car as a battered and bruised Rose stumbled up from the kerb side. John grabbed the keys out of her hand.

Tim got to Rose before she set off after John, and shouted, 'They're not worth it.' So the whole family heard him. Rose was distraught, she'd felt a little secure in the knowledge that those keys meant she could get to her children if she needed to. Without them, she'd be completely locked out of their lives.

Sat in the road crying against Tim's shoulder a feeling of something unknown – a mixture of fear, sickness, and strength – descended over her; she took a deep breath, shook her head, and sprinted towards Darren pushing her terror of him to the back of her mind as she used what strength she had to try to reclaim her keys.

'Give them back, give them back!' she screamed in his face, trying to prise them out of his hand. 'It isn't just your house!' Knowing how pathetic she looked but not caring, she continued to beg for her keys, desperation had taken over. Darren was loving every moment of this, having complete control and power over her.

Rose's tiny frame had no chance against the height and weight of Darren and getting anything from him was impossible, but she had to try. Tim came over, and Darren said, 'Tell her there's no point.'

Tim didn't want to have to say anything, but he did.

'I agree, there is no point – it's only a key. Come on, I'll look after you.' Rose looked at Darren's smirking face with disgust. She'd never looked at him like this before. She'd always smiled through gritted teeth or feigned indifference.

Tim guided her back to the car, but that wasn't the end. Jessica and another sister of Darren's had approached them and started to spit on Rose and Tim like they were the scum of the earth. Rose had never been treated like this, she was mortified and felt degraded.

Darren once again stood back with his arms crossed over his heaving chest as he laughed alongside his sisters.

Rose and Tim finally got into the car and drove off the street. Rose was careful to sit down with all her side stinging and sore. As Tim drove, he saw Darren's family through the rear-view mirror, cheering and jumping like they'd won a huge football match. Neither he nor Rose had seen anything so bizarre before.

As soon as they were out of sight, the tears started, and Rose cried her eyes out. She wailed with pain for her children and disgust at herself for feeling a small amount of relief at finally leaving Darren even if it was like she'd been thrown out as if she was an unruly tenant, at least it was a symbol that the relationship had finally ceased. There was one problem though, she was without her children. Realising that she was sat in a car with her most important possessions, without Millie-Rose and Harrison, with a man she barely knew took its toll. She was inconsolable and told Tim to pull over while she threw up all over the side walk. A headache of epic proportions had settled behind her eyes and she was in a blind panic about her future and whether she'd made the right decision to let Darren have his way.

Tim managed to calm her down after an hour or so and he asked if she wanted to go to the police and report what had happened but, terrified of what Darren might do to the children, she decided against it. Rose needed to get the children back before she confided in the police, but how was this possible now she didn't have the keys to her home?

As soon as they got to Tim's house, Rose ran to the downstairs toilet and was violently sick. Tim, ever the gentleman, looked after her and eventually helped her to bed. No words were shared, he just sat and stroked her hair while she cried herself to sleep.

While Rose slept, Tim was on his laptop working when he decided to Google help for women in domestic abusive relationships. Tim knew that what Darren was doing to her wasn't normal, but he had no idea how to talk to Rose about it, to be able to proceed and get some help. He found the Women's Aid website and within it, a tick box survey.

Rose had told him about some the things that had happened to her, but nothing had prepared him for what he'd just witnessed, and he wasn't convinced that she knew she was in an abusive relationship. Did she think every man behaved like that?

Reading the website, he saw that that was commonplace with victims of abuse – they didn't know what constituted abuse – so he decided that when she woke, he'd ask her to complete the questionnaire so that she could see for herself exactly what had been going on and hopefully, they could start getting her the right help.

Rose was asleep for a few hours but the glow from Tim's MacBook eventually woke her from a shallow sleep. She rubbed her eyes and asked what time it was.

'Don't worry, it's only just gone midnight,' Tim replied, and leant over to give her a kiss on the cheek.

Rose smiled and tried to peak through her eyelashes but the glare from the screen made it impossible.

She snuggled under the duvet and attempting to bring some normalcy to her confused mind, she asked, 'What are you working on at this time of night?'

Tim thought for a moment but decided it was best to be honest and tell Rose what he was doing but he'd paused for too long.

'Well?' Rose asked, her face clouding over as she rubbed her eyes to try to see his screen. Tim put on his business head and got straight to the point, 'I've found this website; why don't you look and do this checklist?' Rose looked at him slightly curious and adjusted her eyes to try to see. She read the header at the top of the webpage: Recognising domestic violence. She looked at Tim.

'Look, I'm not a victim – I can look after myself y—'

'Why don't you sit up and just go through the checklist and take each question one by one and I'll tell you why once you have completed it. Trust me, please.' Tim interrupted.

Rose didn't want to do as Tim had requested but he had been so kind and so she felt obliged, so she sat up and popped her hair back into a pony tail to remove the thick wisps of hair blocking her sight. Rose felt a little nervous and didn't know why but she took a deep breath that she disguised as a sigh and took the MacBook from Tim.

Rose started to go through the checklist:

1. Has your partner tried to keep you from seeing your friends or family? She ticked yes thinking it was OK – some people just want you all for themselves, don't they?

2. Has your partner prevented you course or made it hard for you to start studying, or from going to work? Well, she had to give up work but then set up a business from home so that was different… wasn't it?

3. Does your partner constantly check up on you or follow you? Yes.

4. Does your partner unjustly accuse you of flirting or of having affairs with others? Yes.

5. Does your partner constantly belittle or humiliate you, or regularly criticise or insult you? Yes.

6. Are you ever afraid of your partner? Yes… well these things are always vague, and I mean there're reasons behind it; I think he is just very insecure. She didn't want Tim to be right and was reassuring him that it wasn't that 'type' of relationship. Tim just listened and didn't say a word; he was ready and waiting for her patiently.

7. Have you ever changed your behaviour because you're afraid of what your partner might do or say to you? Yes.

8. Has your partner ever destroyed any of your possessions deliberately? Yes.

9. Has your partner ever hurt or threatened you or your children? Yes.

10. Has your partner ever kept you short of money so you're unable to buy food and other necessary items for yourself and your children or made you take out loans? Well, I guess I'm in debt for a reason, right?

11. Has your partner ever forced you to do something that you really did not want to do? Rose flushed red with this one and didn't want Tim to know why she'd ticked yes.

12. Has your partner ever tried to prevent you from taking necessary medication, or seeking medical help when you felt you needed it? He didn't stop me from getting medication, but he did make me believe I had bipolar and made me seek counselling. I started to doubt myself and did follow his instructions; does that count?

13. Has your partner ever tried to control you by telling you that you could be deported because of your immigration status? Rose felt a bit of relief as she could put a no next to this one.

14. Has your partner ever threatened to take your children away, or said he would refuse to let you take them with you, or even to see them, if you left him? Tears began to fill Rose's big green eyes; had the penny nearly hit the ground?

Breathe.

15. Has your partner ever forced you to have sex with him or with other people? Has he made you participate in sexual activities that you were uncomfortable with?

Tears were now rolling down Rose's face like rain drops sliding down a window pane, she wasn't going to be able to hide it from Tim much longer. He could see the hurt on her face and he knew this was the right thing to have done, he was glad that she was finally seeing the truth and was ready to be a shoulder for her to cry on – any minute.

16. Has your partner ever tried to prevent your leaving the house?

Rose could remember all those time's he'd 'lost' her keys, until one day she found where Darren would put them, so she was unable to leave. Darren had hidden them at the back of the cutlery drawer, the one with all the batteries, screws and rubbish in it. It was left as a plausible explanation if Rose did find the keys. Darren would like to play with her and would shrug it off. 'You silly thing, didn't you remember you put them there?'

At the bottom of the questionnaire it read: *If you answered yes to one or more of the above questions, this indicates that you may be experiencing domestic violence.*

She answered yes to but all but one of the questions! It was too much for Rose to take in. Tim didn't think she'd answer that many yes's and was shocked, he thought from the things she'd already shared with him she'd answer yes to a handful but not this many.

He was trying to stay strong for Rose, but he hadn't realised just how much damage this man had done and was continuing to do to her. Tim held her close as he tried to fight back his own tears. He saw Rose as a perfect mum trying to make a success out of herself even when she was faced with this. Tim didn't think Rose deserved this at all and he didn't know how to help or reassure her that everything was going to be OK, but he had a brainwave. 'I think it's going to be OK, there must be help here locally for victims.'

Rose heard the word victim again and gave another wail of a cry. Tim continued, 'No, I'm serious, there's got to be someone who could help or at least some system; we need to talk to a solicitor.'

Rose's tears of hurt were turning into tears of happiness. It was a most peculiar mixture of emotions, but she couldn't believe that Tim was looking after her and still willing to help after what he'd seen at her house. Rose couldn't fight anymore; she'd done it for six years already and that was more than enough. She just wanted to rest, curl up into a ball and cuddle up in the covers, and hide away from the world.

Tim kept trying to reassure her, 'It's going to be OK; we can draw up a plan on how to sort this out. I'm with you all the way. You do need some rest now though.'

'I can't get any sleep now, all I can think about is everything he's done to me and if he's capable of that, then how on earth am I going to get my kids back? I'm tired, but I am alert, it's hard to explain and I just can't relax.' Rose started to panic. She realised that if Darren was so clever to make her believe their life was 'normal' and alter her perception of what was right, then he was capable of anything.

'Shhhh,' Tim said as he put his finger against her lips, 'you need to calm down, I'm going to make a cup of tea and then we'll put something on the TV; we can get lost in something else for a while.'

Two hours and four episodes of *Friends* later, both were feeling better for the mental break the comedy had given them. When Rose finally fell back to sleep, Tim stayed awake. It was impossible for him to sleep and he didn't want her to wake and not feel comfortable waking him if she needed him.

He had a feeling these next few days were going to be hard.

CHAPTER ELEVEN

Rose woke up at lunchtime the next day with a pounding headache and dry mouth; she hadn't slept this long since before Millie-Rose was born. Next to her, on the bedside table, she saw a glass of fresh orange juice, a glass of water, a cup of tea, and a cup of coffee that Tim had made for her. Rose could hear someone pottering about downstairs and she put on Tim's dressing gown and went to investigate. Tim was cleaning up and had breakfast ready to cook.

'I didn't know what you'd want, so I got everything. Cooked breakfast? Croissants? Cereal?'

Rose blushed and smiled as she looked and saw the selection; she felt an overwhelming sense of gratitude that she was being cared for in this way – it wasn't something she was used to, and she wasn't sure how to respond but decided to kiss him on the cheek. 'What was that for?' he asked.

'For being my hero and pretty much rescuing me.'

'I haven't finished rescuing you yet.'

Tim was saying and doing all the right things to her, but she was wary, Darren had started out this nice and attentive – could she trust Tim the way she had Darren or would it all end in more tears and heartache? She thought this was the real thing, Tim's reaction to yesterday's situation wasn't something that could be faked.

Rose bent over the kitchen counter and grabbed a crumpet; food was a good distraction and hoped it would reduce her headache, she sat at the breakfast bar and Tim waited on her hand and foot and treated her like a princess. Rose couldn't stop herself from smiling even if she was broken on the inside.

Tim thought Rose had woken up a completely different person to the one who fell asleep last night; there was still a deep sadness in her eyes, but she was smiling, and he wondered what had caused it. Surely it wasn't just his breakfast? He sat beside her as she took her time eating her crumpet.

'Are you OK?' he asked with a smile.

'There's a way out, I know there is. What you said last night, well, we can research it can't we?'

Tim was relieved to see a much more determined Rose. 'Of course! Now let's finish our breakfast and then make a start.'

Later, after Rose was dressed and sorted, she seemed to be in a trance and Tim was worried until she asked, 'Could you possibly take me to my dad's? I'm going to have to talk to my family and my dad knows a bit about what's been going on.'

'You don't have to ask. I've taken the rest of the week off work, so I can help you deal with anything that needs to be done.'

They spent the next few hours sorting Rose's things out, and she was feeling a little more relaxed, so they went out to a local pub for dinner that evening. Tim was doing anything to keep her busy and as distracted as possible about the situation. She'd been trying to contact her children all day, but Darren's phone had been switched off. As the day wore on, Tim noticed a significant drop in her mood.

The refreshing spark she'd had when she'd woken had all but disappeared and had been replaced with another emotional headache so when they got back, Tim sent her straight to bed with some painkillers and instructions to get some rest.

The next day they set off on the two-hour journey to Liverpool. It was a cool and chilly day which they both welcomed. Tim noticed that Rose wasn't herself again this morning and was starting to worry about her health.

He didn't add to her troubles by telling her it was his birthday and he'd cancelled all his plans to help her. He didn't want to add to her worries and all he wanted to do was spend it with Rose.

Tim hadn't met a lady like Rose before, all his exes were very self-absorbed in their own lives and expected Tim to buy them expensive gifts and take them on holidays and exotic locations, he often felt like they'd taken advantage of knowing he had some money behind him. Rose was the opposite, she just wanted a normal life, to have a happy and settled family, to live comfortably.

When they arrived in Liverpool, they decided to stop for some lunch at a café Rose used to go to when she lived here. The staff had changed over the years, but Rose was overwhelmed being there. It was over two years since she'd been in Liverpool.

She'd missed her grandfather's funeral, a dear family friend's funeral, and a cousin's wedding too. Rose was starting to realise how isolated she'd become; it was going to take some getting used to being back in contact with family and friends and not having to worry about giving random excuses for missing events or watching her every word in case Darren took it the wrong way.

While they were eating their lunch, the door swung open a Rose was shaken out of her reverie as she heard two familiar voices shrieking her name. Her aunts, Lucy and Laura, were as shocked to see her there as they were excited and once they'd finished hugging her, they squeezed themselves into the empty chairs at the table. It wasn't a question whether they were going to sit with them or not.

Lucy and Laura were often described as the Chuckle Sisters, they were always giggling and cheering everyone up around them; the perfect people to bump into for Rose because it's just what she needed.

Lucy went and ordered them a drink each then rushed back over so she didn't miss any of the conversation. Rose was so excited to see them and immediately felt like she hadn't been away, but she didn't know how she was going to get through the conversation without all the drama being brought up.

'So, are you going to introduce us to your...' Lucy asked, trailing off and coughed mid-sentence, '...friend?' Rose knew full well what the emphasis on *friend* meant.

Rose smiled back and responded, 'Sorry, of course... this is Tim and he's a business connection I made through my company and we're now friends and he's helping me out with some things at the moment.'

Rose realised there was no point keeping anything from them now, so she took a deep breath and began to tell them exactly what Tim was helping her with and why they were in Liverpool today '... so, I guess Tim is keeping me from being homeless right now.'

Rose managed to give them a diluted version of what had been going on and, uncharacteristically they'd sat and listened without interruption… they just drank their coffee while Rose poured out her story to them.

Laura, who worked with the council and knew a fair bit about social services needed to be blunt, she knew it wasn't a situation you let rest but one you needed to act fast on.

'Well, I think my only option is to find a solicitor and fight it in court. I suppose it's why I'm here today too.'

Laura's eyes widened and shook her head. 'No, no, no! Look, what if the courts take months or years and the kids are with him for all that time? You won't have a leg to stand on when it gets to court. You need to get those kids back now before too much time passes, and the courts decide they are settled with their dad.'

Rose hadn't thought about this and she started to panic. 'But, how am I meant to do that? I have no money. I've got £6,000 worth of Darren's debt hanging over me. He was always refused credit and so I took out the loans he needed and now I have nothing I won't be able to get a house.'

She could see how clever Darren had been making her spend her inheritance on furniture and home improvements while he spent his money on going out and computer games. He would only help with the running of the house if he absolutely had to, so the bills had mounted, and they'd fallen behind on the loan repayments, so Rose knew that her credit report badly damaged. He had used money to control her, and she hadn't even realised until now. Rose was holding back her tears, trying to numb herself from the reality of her problems, was she really this venerable and naïve?

'We'll help you,' Laura and Lucy said at the same time,

Tim could see that the whole situation was turning around, but he didn't want Rose to get her hopes up too soon.

'You know I'm here for you too, and I'll help in whatever way I can.'

'Would we be able to live at yours for a bit, Tim? I know it's a lot to ask…' Rose blurted out, immediately realising she shouldn't have done in front of her aunts and putting him on the spot, but it was her only option that she'd thought up.

Tim didn't want to do this now, but he had to. 'The house isn't mine, Rose.'

'Oh?' Rose looked at him in confusion.

'It's not mine, it's my parents' place and they're away now. They get back from holiday in a week. I didn't tell you because I didn't want you to panic about staying over. I'll talk to them about you staying, but I'm not sure they'll be OK with two young kids.'

Tim smiled. 'I will look after you, Rose, I'll help you find a place to live, help you move, and if you want me to stay with you for a bit, then I will do that; I'm here for you. It may not be as easy as you originally thought but there is always an answer.'

Rose had told him she was afraid to be on her own in a house in case Darren came to find her.

Lucy and Laura were whispering to each other and Tim was holding Rose's hand trying to reassure her. He could see that her mind was spinning again, and that there were thoughts running through her head uncontrollably.

'I'm happy to give you £500 to help towards a deposit on a house and I have some furniture that you're welcome to have,' Laura said.

Rose almost choked on her drink and then Lucy piped up, 'I'm going to match it with another £500 so that should be enough for a deposit and I have some cutlery and other bits you're welcome to.'

Rose couldn't hold back the tears any longer, 'I can't take money off you. I haven't seen you in two years! Why would you do that?' Everyone in the café looked at them as Tim put his arm around her and passed her a serviette to dry her tears.

Laura spoke again, 'Look, we know why you haven't seen us, and nothing changes the fact that you're our family; those kids need to be with you.' Both her aunts got their cheque books out and each wrote Rose a cheque for £500. Lucy and Laura were devastated that their niece was in this situation, but the look on her face as they handed over their cheques was all they needed to know; that Rose would be able to get through this even if it was a longer road to take. There was a new spark in her eyes that shone out with hope.

It was like a pressure had been released and they caught up on other aspects of each other's lives before Rose decided she needed to go and see her dad. Promising to keep in touch with them, she said goodbye to her aunts by giving them a big squeeze of a hug and followed Tim out the door and back to the car.

Watching her while he was driving out of the corner of his eye, Tim saw a glow to her face that he'd never seen before. Tim for the first time felt a wave of relief.

'Oh my gosh, Tim, can you believe it! I really wasn't expecting that. I really can get the kids back and get out of this for good now. I don't care what my mum or dad say because, at last, I feel like I'm getting somewhere. Did that really just happen?' Rose was thinking about it all, replaying her aunt's actions in her head as they drove along. She was overwhelmed with love and gratitude that they'd just given her.

Rose's dad, Alfie, was in his late fifties and lived in a third-floor apartment, which he referred to as his penthouse. He was obsessed with technology but never knew how to work it properly meaning he was always getting someone round to reset it or fix it.

When he opened the door, Rose was comforted to see that he was wearing his standard outfit of jeans and shirt, his black hair was flecked with more grey than the last time she'd seen him, and his brown framed glasses were perched on the end of his nose as usual.

It had been two years since they'd seen each other but that didn't change the fact that she'd always be his little girl and it was as if they'd seen each other just the other day.

Rose introduced Tim and although wary, her father welcomed them in and settled them on the sofa while he made them all a latte on his new coffee machine, chocolate sprinkles included.

Alfie cut to the chase. 'So, go on then, you only come over if something's happened?' He listened without interruption as Rose explained the whole story. Although Alfie knew snippets from the snatched phone calls they'd had over the last two years, he was shocked to hear the rest of it.

'I did tell you to have a long engagement. I always thought Darren was weird and even though I don't talk to your mother, I know she did too... I guess you didn't have much choice, but it looks like Tim is bringing my daughter back home,' Alfie said as he smiled at him in thanks. 'I'm happy to match your aunties and give you £500 too by the way.'

'Oh, Dad...' Rose sighed and cried into his shoulder as she leant to hug him.

Alfie was a no-nonsense kind of guy and didn't hold back. 'Tim, I expect you to look after her.' His stern look said that he was serious and there was an expectation there.

Just half hour later and they were on the way back to York, Rose was talking ten to the dozen about what had happened and was getting tired from repeating herself. After all these years of worry about her family not wanting to know her because of the things Darren had made her do, isolating herself from them, all it had taken was for her to reach out and they were there. They still loved her and that meant the world to her.

As she started to fall asleep in the car, it flashed through her mind that no one was thinking about how hard it would be to get the children back from Darren, he wasn't going to just hand them over, they were all the power he had left over her and he wouldn't give that up without a fight, but the thought didn't hold for long as exhaustion won once again and Rose drifted into the first naturally peaceful sleep she'd had for weeks.

* * *

The next couple of weeks were spent in a blur of paperwork and information gathering – from solicitor's documents to police record numbers to new house details. They had found a house in Liverpool close where Rose's family lived that looked perfect for what they needed. She knew she needed to be there so that she had their support and that she'd be as far away from Darren as she could be at this point in the process.

Tim had decided that he was going to move over with her for a while, they'd started to become dependent on each other and his feelings for her were deepening. He was starting to see a completely different side to her now that she was away from Darren and recovering with the ability to be able to rest.

And, although she'd split up with him a few months ago, the fact that they had lived together had always made Darren think they might get back together. Now though, he knew exactly where he stood with Rose and although he'd never push her, he knew he wanted a future with her.

CHAPTER TWELVE

Christmas Eve soon arrived, and Rose, like most other mothers in the world, was looking forward to the special plans she'd made for her and her children. Eating the last chocolate in the calendar, putting the carrots and biscuits out for Santa and Rudolph. Getting snuggled and watching their favourite Christmas movies with hot chocolate and marshmallows.

She desperately hated those few seconds that had plagued her mornings since she'd been thrown out. Those seconds lulled her into thinking she would open her eyes and see her babies on her bed, jumping around, or that she'd hear Millie-Rose telling Harrison a story through the open bedroom doors.

Instead, this Christmas Eve, she was waking up on Lyndsey's lumpy sofa with the hangover from hell and no to give her a much-needed cuddle.

Darren had thrown her out three weeks ago and she'd been staying with Tim. However, Darren was now being awful and would only let her have the children for hours on Christmas Day. She knew Tim had plans with his family, so she didn't tell him what was going on as she knew he'd change his plans to be with her.

There was no way, after everything he'd done for her, she was going to let him ruin his day.

Rose desperately missed her children and couldn't face being alone last night. Armed with wine she'd arrived at Lindsey's and even though it had been almost a year since they'd seen each other, it felt like no time had passed. Lindsey fell back into the caring role, wanting to help any way she could. Having recently lost a dear friend she wanted nothing more than Rose to be happy.

Last week Darren had taken the last of her money to pay the rent and bills. Rose willingly paid it after all, she was living rent free and wouldn't risk the children being homeless. Even after she'd done that, yesterday Darren had told Rose that she was only allowed to see them for two hours on Christmas Day.

She'd been devastated, she was their mother, it was Christmas Day... two hours was not enough!

Feeling ill, the combination of a hangover and stress taking its toll on her, Rose crawled to the kitchen to get some water and to look for Lindsey, but she wasn't in. Getting to the bathroom just in time, Rose threw up into the toilet. Her head was pounding, and with squinted eyes she had a root around the bathroom cabinet and discovered packets and packets of Paracetamol.

Her thoughts wandered... she hadn't spent any real time with her children for weeks, she had no idea what Tim thought about her, she didn't have a home, she had no money, and she was terrified the bank were going to be calling her about the debts building up, she daren't look at her phone.

Alone.

Isolated.

Everything in her life that had once kept her going was now gone.

The lowest place she could imagine was her reality.

Before she knew it, she'd taken thirty tablets and repeated history.

They slid down her throat like Tic-Tacs.

She knew Darren would have a hold over her for the rest of her life, was it better just suffering than for him to use the children like this?

She'd promised herself she'd never do this again, she'd remain strong, she'd remain firm, so the children had her. But the children didn't have her now and the fear of what was going to come was enough to force her hand.

She was about to pop some more from their packet when her phone buzzed. Rose pulled it out and looked at the screen saver – her beautiful children's faces were staring back at her and she saw there were loads of missed calls and messages off Tim.

Rose glanced in the mirror and saw herself staring back, pale, taut, hair a mess, mascara smudged, and about to have more Paracetamol to kill herself.

What the fuck? I have to stop this! Snap out of it! Was I really going to let Darren win? He would have loved this outcome, wouldn't he?

The messages from Tim were surprising; he'd changed his plans to be with her and was desperately trying to get in touch to let her know, he wanted her, her children wanted her, they needed her!

Like history playing out, Rose made herself throw up again and brought up as much as she could manage. Her throat was sore from the continued attempts and until she was satisfied her stomach was empty, she stood up with a renewed energy and determination to sort everything out.

* * *

It was a warm Christmas Day and the two precious hours she'd had with the children went too fast and she left with her spirits in tatters. She'd booked into a small, cheap hotel for a couple of nights. Rose tried her utmost not to cry and held her breath not to let a single tear drop fall; she couldn't face another sobbing session and pushing down the lump in her throat was draining her.

'Merry Christmas to me,' Rose said aloud as she stared at the magnolia wall. Millie-Rose kept asking her when they could stay with her or when she'd be coming back. Harrison wouldn't leave her side and was very quiet and solemn.

Rose had an ache in her heart the whole time and they lapped up every moment of their two hours together, they didn't see the broken TV, the hair in the drain, the cobwebs in the corners of the room, or the line of dust on the surfaces and windowsills. They didn't notice the yellow net curtains in the window or the stained bedsheets or the scum that circled the sink.

They were focused on their mummy and being together in their bubble where they were really in a living room with an open fire staying warm, the Christmas tree was well dressed, and heaps of presents underneath it, they all sat on the fluffy rug wearing matching pyjamas and slippers on to match.

If Rose was honest, it was the worst Christmas she'd ever had. Barely any gifts as money was so tight and had been soaked up by the hotel room plus the grand she'd given Den. Struggling to gather funds, she managed to get some beautiful gifts from the charity shops in town. Having little experience with them in the past, she hadn't known what to expect but was so happy with her purchases. She needn't have worried though, they didn't need many gifts, they spent the whole time hugging Rose close, that's all they really wanted – their mummy.

All too soon it was time to take them back. Rose thought about keeping them with her, but she knew Darren would come after her and she couldn't keep them in a single bed hotel room. Harrison's asthma would cause him difficulties if he stayed much longer so Rose reluctantly dropped them back off. Darren had a huge grin on his face when she arrived, and he looked like a pig in shit, he was having his moment.

Rose returned to the hotel slowly, she had nothing to rush for. Rose went in with her head down, unlocked the door to her room, and shut it behind her before crumbling to the floor like someone had cut her puppet strings.

And she wept.

Her heart was breaking, being smashed and ripped into little pieces, then stamped on.

She tried to tell herself it was going to be OK, tried to remain positive, but how was it going to be OK?

Half an hour later she was still sobbing on the floor, every time she thought the last tear had fallen, the sheer desperation of the situation flooded over her again and more tears appeared. Wishing she was a drinker with a huge bottle of vodka to hand, she eventually dragged herself off the floor and to the bed. If she was going to cry herself to sleep, she might as well do it on the lumpy bed instead of the cold, hard floor.

A knock on the door startled her and thinking it was someone at the wrong room, she splashed some water on her face in the bathroom and went to send them away. But it wasn't a stranger. Rose couldn't believe it.

'You're meant to be with your family,' she whispered.

Tim simply smiled and said, 'No one deserves to be alone on Christmas Day, especially you.'

Her knight in shining armour had arrived at the perfect moment to rescue her, again.

He looked at Rose like she was the most beautiful woman in the world when Rose felt she looked considerably less than that. It shouldn't have been important given the circumstances but right then, for her, it was. It was really important. He made Rose feel something other than desolate, something more than the mess she saw. He looked at her in a way that made her know completely that she was important. She was safe.

He told her to get dressed – they were going out for Christmas dinner.

Rose didn't argue, she couldn't, so she did as he asked. He didn't rush her, she slapped on as much make-up as she could, so it hid the dark puffy circles under her eyes and take away the washed-out ghost look she'd adopted.

When she emerged from the bathroom wearing the only dress she had with her which she'd baby-wiped clean, the look on Tim's face told her everything she needed to know about him.

'Thank you,' she whispered as she sat on the edge of the bed to put her shoes on.

Tim raised one eyebrow, knelt down to her eye level and looked at her straight in the eyes and said firmly, 'First of all you don't need to thank me and second, I said I will help you and I mean that. I don't offer help lightly.'

Rose tried to interrupt but Tim put his pointed finger to

her lips and said to her, 'Please listen to me: you're welcome to stay here, and I don't just mean tonight but if you need to come and stay for a few weeks or months, even if it's to have a break from him. I don't have a big family and I get pretty lonely – I'm guessing you know how that feels? I've got to be honest, I've never done this before but there's something about you that makes me want to help and I'm concerned about you. You have my number and you never have to worry about what I'm doing, just ring.'

Rose couldn't believe what she was hearing and kept feeling that she didn't want to go back at all; it felt nice to feel cared for.

Tim continued, 'Can I ask you something?' Rose nodded at him, wondering what he was going to ask. 'What on earth were you doing with someone like him? I mean I can tell just from meeting you on a couple of occasions that you're not stupid.'

Rose let out a sigh and wondered how she was going to answer that question.

'I can't say I was stupid, and I can't say I was clever because honestly, I didn't expect to get into this situation, I don't really know how it's gone this far without me realising exactly what was happening. I don't see myself as a victim – I just see fault and blame on my part for not getting out sooner.

'But the thing is, Tim, I was scared. In the end *he* ended the relationship with me because I found out about him sleeping with someone else and he blamed me for finding out. It was only a few months ago, and I hadn't long since met you. I know when I met him he used to say such wonderful things about me; he used to spoil me, take me shopping, wine and dine me and honestly, you wouldn't think anything of it.

'It didn't take me long to realise I'd made the wrong decision and by then I was stuck – miles away from my family with my name on a tenancy agreement. How was I supposed to get out?'

Tim was watching Rose struggle to answer the question and offered to help. 'I think you'll find I *can* understand, but I *won't* until I live it *with* you. I wanted to ask because I want you to know that you won't see that behaviour from me. OK... I may spoil you, wine and dine you, but I don't plan to stop that, and I don't plan to isolate you – in fact I want the opposite of that.'

Tim smiled at Rose and lifted her chin with his finger she was looking into his eyes; he wanted her to see that they showed he was serious and that he will protect her.

Tears filled her eyes as she understood the intensity and honesty of his words. Tim kissed the top of her forehead. Rose didn't know what to say, and she was desperately trying not to let a single tear drop from the pools in her eyes.

Rose took a risk by leaning towards Tim for a kiss but as she was sat with her lips pursed waiting and her palms becoming hot, she was feeling very nervous. Until at last, she felt Tim's lips slowly kiss her back. His hands ran through her hair and he held her head gently pulling her closer to him. She was overcome with an unfamiliar sensation of butterflies in her tummy and her heart was now racing. She knew Tim wasn't a quivering wreck like her but a handsome man that had chosen her.

They'd been kissing for what seemed like hours and the intensity was building, Rose was feeling more and more nervous and light-headed; as she'd only slept with Darren and one other man her confidence almost didn't exist in this department. Tim pulled her closer.

She felt so hot she thought she needed to get some cool

air; Tim, on the other hand, showed no nerves but oozed sexiness. They had reached the point of no return and Rose knew there and then that she could easily fall for this guy.

Laid in his arms after, Rose heard him whisper, 'I love you.'

She believed him.

* * *

A week had gone by and things had started to feel unsettled and concerning for Rose as Den had stopped messaging her.

Rose knew that in times of silence there was reason to be concerned.

Due to have the children on New Year's Eve, Rose went to pick them up. The door was opened by a dirty man with a fag hanging from his mouth and his hand in his pants, he smelt of booze, BO, and sewers.

The children came to see her looking like they'd been in the same clothes since she dropped them off on Christmas Day. Running to her, they squealed with joy when she pulled them bot in to an embrace and swung them around in the garden.

Den grunted at her, 'You have an hour today.' And slammed the door in their faces. He didn't even say goodbye to his children.

Rose hurried them into the car and drove them back to the hotel. She put them straight into the bath, found they both had rashes, dirt under their nails, blood-shot eyes, and were just grotty. Rose didn't know what to do or what to think. It was so close to moving day, but she was worried about the kids even more. Rose had to take action and had to talk to the police, Tim and she were trying to manage the situation, but it had gotten further out of hand. Unexpectedly and concerning.

The police became heavily involved in the situation when one night, Rose finally picked up the phone and decided to tell them all about what had happened including how she was forced out of her home and spat on. Tim was there right beside her with his hand on her lap, rubbing her thigh gently as she was gasping and trying to get out her words. At first, she spoke clearly but as she came to the end of the story and talked about the children, Rose felt a pain in her gut and an ache in her heart.

She'd spent an hour attempting to log it on the phone and in the end, the police arranged for her to come to the station to make an official statement and go through the full story. It wasn't a simple complication, it was a deep-rooted problem with lots of events that came together to make a bigger picture. The police could tell that Rose was in distress and to be able to help her it was important to gain an understanding of everything that had happened.

Walking into the police station less than half an hour later, Rose felt degraded, she couldn't understand why she felt so ashamed to be there. Never needing the police before it was all very unsettling, but those feelings had to be put aside. The two officers behind reception were having a giggle and not looking at them, one officer spoke. 'Sorry, yes... how can I help?'

Coughing and then looking up at them, Rose mumbled that she'd been directed by 101, and the officer could see her bright-red, blood-shot eyes, rosy cheeks, and the scrunched-up tissue in her hand. Tim placed his arm around her waist.

'What she's trying to say is that we rang 101, and they said to come in and issue a statement, there should be a note on the computer system about it?'

Rose was relieved Tim had managed to explain it properly, she could barely get her words out.

Time stood still while they waited for the officer to locate their notes and get an officer to come and see them. Every second felt like a minute and Rose still had of tears running down her cheeks and down her neck. Tim couldn't stop checking his watch and could feel Rose shaking next to him.

At the left side of the reception a door finally opened, and an officer invited them to follow her through. Ushered to some little sofas just through the door, Rose and Tim sat down. The sofa's looked like they belonged in a doctors' surgery with their surgical green colour. A small coffee table sat in the middle which reminded Rose of a school table that had its legs cut in half.

'I'm PC Samson, how can I help you today?' The officer started.

Rose was taken a back about how it went straight to the point and PC Samson had this hard face with her black fringe hiding the tops of her eyes. There was a pause as Rose collected her thoughts and tried to take a couple of deep breathes.

'I… erm… a couple of weeks ago… I was forced to leave my own home by my husband…' deep breath '…he wasn't nice to me before that… but anyway… he made sure I knew that this wasn't going to be the end as he had all of his family there, his sister followed me around the house as I tried to get some things and when I went back to the car I was asked to give him the keys. I didn't want to because I was worried for my children and thought I could get them at some time or something I don't really know…'

'…and I… I… I tried to get the keys… I couldn't get them…' overcome with the enormity of it all, she put her head in her hands.

'I'm so stupid!'

Tim rubbed her back, but it didn't do anything, the police officer said she'd get a tissue and while she was gone, Tim tried to comfort Rose.

'This is the best thing you can do, you'll feel better once you've told the police everything.'

Rose knew he was right and just having him by her side was enough to help her regain a small amount of control. PC Samson returned with a box of tissues, took one out, and passed it to Rose,

'I think we should go somewhere a little more private, follow me and I will help as much as I can, OK?' There was some empathy in PC Samson's voice and she ushered them to a little room around the corner.

PC Samson sat down on the opposite side of the table and reassured them.

'I think it would help you a little if we were in here as it's a bit quieter and we won't be disturbed. I know we're behind a desk here and not on the sofas but it's nothing to worry about. Is that OK?' Rose nodded, and Tim thought it was time he broke the ice and mention what he'd witnessed and experienced, hoping it would give the officer a bit more of the picture.

'I've only known Rose for around eight months...' And he told the officer everything he had seen so far.

He continued, 'Since she was forced out of her home, she has had no help from the housing association, local solicitors charge and offer no free consultations to someone without money, social services haven't been helpful as they don't think the children are in danger from their father, and so Rose is staying with me because no one is willing to house a single woman with no children.

We're here today because Rose is planning to take the

children to her new house near Liverpool on one of the 'access' days Darren has assigned to her. Obviously, he doesn't know but they need to be with their mum. Harrison, her youngest, isn't well, and he is being neglected. Darren isn't even looking after them most of the time – they're being passed around people they don't know.'

Rose looked up at Tim's serious face as he got everything off his chest, he was determined to get some help and support for her. How could Rose have done this without him, she had no voice, no place, and no identity.

PC Samson thought for a moment, blew her fringe so she could look at the notes she'd taken, and started to go through the list of questions she'd made.

'First, I need to take some details about you and Darren, if you could give me your full name, date of birth, and address; and the same for Darren please.'

It had just become official and Rose started to mumble her answers, it followed with a lengthy interrogation; challenging her decisions and asking why she hadn't left before he threw her out. Why did she deal with it for all this time? What led him to do this and that. It was becoming more and more apparent that PC Sampson thought Rose should have done things differently, that she should have been a better mum; this wasn't news to her, she'd asked herself the same questions over and over, before and after leaving Darren.

But now, she had the answers. Now she wasn't going to let anyone, not even a police officer, make her feel any guiltier than she'd made herself. For the first time since walking through the station door, she spoke with confidence and determination.

'I didn't ask for this, when I met him he didn't come with a label on telling me what the ingredients where and would leave me with more than food poisoning. There was nothing I could do to please him, I was wiped of all emotions and living like a robot.

'I didn't want this, I didn't ask for this and if it was my choice, if it was only me I had to think about I would have left years ago but it wasn't safe, and it wasn't just me, and I had no money. Where do you go when you have no one? Live on the streets? It's only thanks to Tim that I'm not living on the streets as no one else offered any help!'

Almost depleted after her rant, she didn't know where to look.

'All I want to know is will I be in trouble for taking the children on my access day? I know he will ring the police and say I've kidnapped them – is it kidnap? I thought getting it on record would stop any searches or anything...' she eventually whispered into the shocked silence.

PC Samson wiggled her bum to the back of her seat and let out a little cough before she continued to speak.

'The only reason we ask these questions is so we can get an idea of what he is like and build a picture about your situation. I understand coming here today has taken a lot from you...' She handed Rose a tissue as tears started to fall again.

'We will help you and I will run through my thoughts in a moment. I just want to go and check with my sergeant that my advice is correct, and it would help you. We have to make sure your children are safe and that you are as well. If you could just give me a few minutes I'll be as quick as I can, OK?'

Rose nodded and blew her nose; the box of tissues had been well used, and she'd taken the last one.

'I'll get another box of tissues as well.' And she left the room.

Tim and Rose waited in silence, both lost in their own anxious thoughts.

When Sampson finally returned, they were barely breathing.

Amazingly, she confirmed that their plan was OK. All Rose had to do was attend the local station in Liverpool when they arrived and present them with the children's birth certificates and her ID to prove she was their mother, and everything would be OK.

Darren could claim they'd been kidnapped all he wanted but this was all going on the police database so as soon as he made the call, their names would come up and the police would do nothing so long as Rose called Darren after she'd left with the children to tell him they were with her and were safe.

All Rose had to do now was put her plan into action.

Simple... Right?

CHAPTER THIRTEEN

They were starting to feel the pressure as the plans came together. Rose had spent a lot of money getting everything in place, right down to the time the removal van they'd hired would be arriving at each of her relative's homes to collect the furniture they were giving her.

Tim, however, was feeling very anxious that Darren would somehow find out what they were planning. Rose couldn't sleep and all she kept on doing was going through the plan over and over so it was memorised and so she was fully prepared.

First: get everything in to the new house. Second: stay over that night and set up the donated furniture and get the house as ready as possible going back to Tim's parents' house the following evening. Third: collect the children as normal on the Saturday and take them straight to the new house in Liverpool.

It was simple as 1,2,3 but everyone knew that this could all go wrong and collapse in on itself.

The night before they were due to collect the children, Tim's mum, Sarah, had cooked up a huge feast. She and

Rose adored each other and had become close over the last few weeks. Although grateful for the effort Sarah had gone to, Rose was too anxious to eat. They had gone over every possible outcome for the next couple of days and were as confident as they could be that they had it all worked out until Rose's phone beeped a text message had arrived.

Hi Rose, I don't think Harrison is well enough to see you tomorrow as he has got worse this last week. Millie-Rose could come, and Harrison could stay with me.

'He knows our plan! Why would he not allow Harrison to see me, it'll make him feel better? You told me that this would happen, Tim, that he'd try to control me again… that's it, the plan has gone down the pan.' Tim was rubbing her back while Sarah went to make her a cup of tea and get her a glass of water.

Eventually calming down, Rose listened to reason – James, Tim's dad, reminded her that she'd taken Harrison to the doctor a couple of weeks ago and she should explain to Darren that she was more than capable of handling anything that needed to be done if he got really poorly.

There were a few nerve-wracking minutes as responses flew back and forth and Rose was glued to her phone as if no one else was around, waiting for the next beep. Eventually Darren said he'd see how Harrison was in the morning and would let her know if she could take him or not.

Rose barely slept that night worrying about it all going wrong, but finally the day had come, and Rose drove her old, green, Ford Fiesta to collect her children. Her heart was racing, and she'd already been sick twice before setting off.

Tim was back at his parents' house and was talking to her over hands-free to calm her down. Beads of sweat trickled down her clammy face, all she had to do was get through the next few minutes without giving the game away, could she put on this front and could she manage her nerves?

Before Rose drove on to the street, she set her phone to record in her pocket; she did this every time she saw Darren now to keep track if anything was said or done. Being near him was hard enough without having to remember all the things he said to her.

She took one last breath as she pulled up in front of her old home and with all the fake confidence she could muster, she opened her car door and walked up the driveway. She'd made a bit of an effort today and had her hair down and had tried to cover the fact that her skin seemed to have turned a yellowy-green colour and she'd lightened the dark circles around her eyes. She didn't want the children to see their mummy like that.

The front door opened as she approached and when Millie-Rose, stood with her rucksack on and a huge smile, saw Rose, she almost knocked her to the ground when she ran and threw herself into a tight hug. Rose secured Millie-Rose in her pink car seat and then went to get Harrison. Rose couldn't believe it, he was in Darren's arms and looked seriously unwell.

His eyes were gluey and nearly sealed shut, his cheeks were red, but the rest of his face was pale and washed out. When he saw Rose, he wriggled out of his dad's arms and climbed over to Rose, but she could see his whole body was weak. As soon as she held him, he wept and snuggled into her neck to smell her; his favourite position for comfort.

'So, have you taken him to the doctor's?' she asked Darren.

'No, you know how these bug things are, they clear up in no time.'

Rose held her tongue and thought about the end goal which was now in sight. 'What medicine has he had this morning, so I know when to give him some more?'

'None yet, I was going to mention to you he needs some.'

Rose had heard enough and put Harrison in the car with his comfort blanket and he managed to calm down, but he felt extremely hot to touch. She told the kids to say goodbye, but they weren't interested. Harrison didn't bother waving and Millie-Rose was more concerned to find out what they were going to be doing and telling Rose she'd been playing doctor to try make Harrison better.

Rose drove away and loved the feeling; *she was* going to make Harrison better, and *she was* going to give them a happy life and love and care for them like she'd been yearning to do for these last few long weeks.

Rose phoned Tim on the loudspeaker to let him know that it had gone smoothly, and she was coming to pick him up and 'zoom, zoom.'

Millie-Rose was talking away in the background and poor Harrison was cuddling his blanket while smiling at his mummy through the rear-view mirror, he really didn't look well. 'We're going to have to go straight to the hospital, Harrison is really not well,' Rose told Tim when she picked him up.

He took one look at Harrison and jumped into the car. 'We'll have to drive to Liverpool hospital because if he's admitted here, who knows what will happen?' Tim told her. As awful as that felt to them both, they knew it was the right thing to do. They weren't planning on telling Darren where in the country they were going so he wouldn't be able to hijack them at the hospital.

Rose set off and by his feet, Tim could see a plastic bag with some Fruit Shoots, sandwiches, bananas, apples, and some chocolate buttons in it and smiled at how prepared Rose was for everything.

The journey felt never-ending. They could hear Harrison wheezing and Millie-Rose was concerned too as he wasn't talking to her. Rose told her the plan, and that they were going to stay with Mummy and Tim for now and would get a doctor to look at Harrison.

Millie-Rose was thrilled with the idea of living with Mummy and Tim.

'I'm so excited, can I stay with you forever?'

Rose knew she couldn't answer yet because who knew what was going to happen next. She desperately wanted to shout yes and reassure Millie-Rose, but she didn't want to lie to her daughter.

Two hours passed, and they'd just gone through the Birkenhead tunnel when they saw a police station and Rose pulled in.

'We'd better do this first to save our own backs, we don't know what's going to happen at the hospital.'

Rose left Tim and the children in the car and walked up to the entrance, pressed the buzzer, and waited for an answer. Time practically stood still like it did when they were at the station in York, Rose was trying to hold herself together, not let the guilt take over.

I should have been stronger, I should have demanded to stay with Millie-Rose and Harrison or demanded they come with me. Why couldn't I do it? Why did he take over like he did? Rose was daydreaming with a stern face with all the questions and thoughts she had rushing around her head.

Five minutes later and a voice sounded through the speaker, 'Yes, how can we help?'

Rose came out of her trance and didn't know where to start.

'Erm… well… you see, I have my two children in the car,

I've picked them up from their dad's, but I don't plan on taking them back. It's kind of a long story, and, erm, oh yeah, the Yorkshire police have assisted me, and I have some reference numbers I can give you.'

There was a loud sigh, and the voice replied, 'There will be someone with you shortly.'

Another long five minutes went by.

Rose looked over to the car and could see Tim handing the kids a Fruit Shoot each and it seemed there was no reason to worry just yet. A middle-aged, blonde police officer came to the doors and said, 'I'm with the traffic department but I'm going to make some checks on the log numbers you have, if that's OK?' And she ushered Rose into the entrance hall.

Rose nervously replied, 'Thank you so much; the police in Yorkshire said to hand ourselves over, so to speak, so you're prepared at this end in case their dad rings up later. There's something else though, my son is very ill, and I need to take him to hospital as soon as I can. I would have gone there first, but I knew I had to do this as we may be at the hospital for hours.'

'Where are the children now?'

'Outside in the car with my friend waiting for me.'

She popped her head outside the entrance and could see the three of them waiting in the car parked closest.

'OK, I'll log this now and you head to the hospital. If there's any more information we need we'll get in touch; I'm assuming all your contact details are on the log files?' she asked.

'Yes, they are,' Rose replied as she shuffled in her bag, 'and here are their birth certificates if you need them?'

The officer smiled at Rose and took the certificates out of her hand. 'I'll photocopy these and log it so it's on file, do you have any ID on you as well? I will take that down.'

Rose rushed through her purse and handed over her driver's license. While Rose waited for her to come back, she sent a text to Tim asking, *Is everything OK? Nearly done and then we can shoot off xx.*

Kids are fine, don't worry, just concentrate on this part and then we can get onto the next x.

Surprisingly, the police officer was really quick and handed the certificates back to Rose and wished her well. It was nice to not feel the judgement she'd expected; Rose felt ashamed even to have to be in the police station and 'hand herself over' for being with her own children.

Getting back in the car, Rose said, 'Now, let's get Harrison to the hospital, shall we? You're doing a good job of looking after him, Millie.' She turned to look at Tim. 'And so are you,' she said with a smile.

Millie-Rose grinned with pride and Rose grinned back thinking what a credit her children were to her.

Rose looked over at a now sleeping Harrison who was snorting each time he breathed in.

Tim reassured her, 'They've been fine, we've been singing different songs together, and Millie-Rose has been teaching me some new ones. But come on, let's get going. I'll drive, so let's swap places.'

It wasn't long before they'd arrived at the hospital, parked in the car park, and hurried into A&E. Rose was carrying Harrison like he was the most precious thing in the whole world concern for his condition deepening with every passing second. They signed in at the reception and Rose explained what was wrong but told the receptionist that if anyone rang the hospital asking about Harrison, not to confirm that he was there.

Finally, they sat down and waited. Millie-Rose stuck to

her mum like a leech and Rose felt sick at the emotional strain she could see in her little face.

As they waited, and the guilt started to build that she hadn't been there for Harrison sooner started to build, the thoughts of what he had been through before made Rose feel a regret that she hadn't got out sooner.

* * *

Rose was daydreaming and didn't hear the nurse when she called out Harrison's name. Tim had to give her a nudge. Rose got up in a rush and ushered the kids into the cubicle to be seen.

The nurse was young and could see Harrison wasn't well at all and Rose gave her all the information she knew about his condition while she carried out a full examination of Harrison and asked if he had any allergies before giving him some Paracetamol. She asked for them to sit in the waiting room again for the doctor.

They barely had a chance to sit back down before the doctor called Harrison's name. Rose knew it must be something serious as she'd never heard of people being called this quickly before.

They headed into another cubicle and the doctor asked for Harrison to be stripped down to his nappy for his assessment. As the doctor checked him over, Rose repeated her story with her head hanging in shame. The doctor said that Harrison would have to be admitted to the ward overnight. He confirmed he had severe conjunctivitis, a chest infection, and an ear infection, all of which had got out of control.

The doctor was kind reassuring, but Rose felt this huge guilt that she'd let her baby boy get so ill.

The doctor checked his oxygen levels, and they were down in the sixties '...the normal level should be at least ninety-five,' he informed them.

Rose burst into tears and Tim took over asking the doctor all the necessary questions. She held Harrison close and thanked God that they had this plan in place and were able to get Harrison the medical attention he needed. What would have happened if it was any longer?

That night, Harrison was admitted to a ward; they'd been at the hospital for hours now and Millie-Rose was getting tired and bored; she'd been so well behaved all this time.

Harrison needed help with his oxygen levels, but he refused to put on the mask. The nurse tried to change it to one that goes into the nose, but Harrison was distraught and made himself sick. In the end, Tim sat Harrison on his knee and held the mask until he fell asleep and would then put him in the cot.

Rose was so grateful that even though they'd only met a few times, her children had instantly taken to Tim, and he to them. It helped that she could entertain Millie-Rose while Tim looked after Harrison.

The children eventually fell asleep while sat on their knees, but Tim and Rose were less than comfortable in the hard-plastic chairs. With Harrison where he was, Tim was able to hold the mask close to his face to help his oxygen levels while Rose managed to get them a movie to watch on her phone.

The nurses came to check up on Harrison throughout the night, adding to the anxiety Rose was already feeling. She noticed that they weren't doing this with the other children on the ward – were they being scrutinised closely because of the circumstances of Harrison's deterioration?

The next three days were a blur of doctors, nurses, tests,

and sleep deprivation. Harrison started to improve on some levels, but his oxygen wouldn't stabilise, so he was kept in. Between them, Tim and Rose shared the care and Millie-Rose was invited to stay with Lucy and Laura when they were able to help out.

Along with the conjunctivitis, Harrison was diagnosed with bronchitis and asthma. Rose was devastated that in the few weeks she'd been away, these had been ignored to the point her son was hospitalised. Her guilt levels were sky-high, and she didn't sleep any better or even feel safe, she was constantly looking over her shoulder just in case Darren was going to turn up out of the blue. The doctors finally gave them Harrison's discharge note, and it noted that his illnesses were due to neglect.

While they were in the hospital, Rose had booked an appointment with a local solicitor, so she could start the divorce proceedings. She desperately wanted to be released from Darren and to feel free and not under his control. She didn't want to have his surname any longer.

Rose was starting to realise that life wasn't normal with Darren and it had dawned on her just how bad her life was and how she felt trapped, imprisoned, isolated, intimidated, and manipulated. Luckily, she'd managed to find a solicitor who offered a free half hour consultation, so she'd be able to find out what the process for starting a divorce was. It was going to be expensive, and she didn't know how she'd pay for it, but she needed to at least start.

That afternoon, after Harrison was settled at the new house, Rose went to the solicitor's office while Tim looked after the children, he was becoming a natural and got on well with Rose's family who would drop by with odd bits and bobs they would buy. Tim had also made changes to his business and was going to be taking on personal assistant so that he could delegate his work when the time came to return to work, he hadn't bothered Rose with the details of the background tasks Tim was doing because he felt it was imperative for her to focus on herself and the children.

Rose was sat in the waiting room and filled out the solicitor's enquiry form, wondering if there could be an easy resolution to this car crash of a mess.

It seemed to take some time for the solicitor to call her through so while she waited, she did some quick networking on different social media platforms for her business. Rose was a natural worrier and knew that Tim was giving up a lot of his time to be with her. His business must be suffering. She'd tried to talk to him about it, but he wouldn't hear of it and told her not to think about it.

An email pinged up and Rose's heart dropped when she saw the sender... Darren. There was nothing in the body of the email, just an attachment. When it downloaded, Rose nearly passed out as she read it:

York County Court and Family Court. The court orders that: 1. The applications for a Residence Order and the return of the children to the Applicant's care be listed at York County Court.

Rose was shaking, and nausea flowed through her body. She read further down and saw the hearing was set for Monday – it was now Friday afternoon – 'Feck,' she said out loud and thought it was bloody good luck she was waiting to see a solicitor. Rose was trying to understand the legal jargon when she heard her name, looking up, she saw a tall, slim brunette with black, thick-rimmed glasses perched on the end of her nose. Rose felt like she was at school and had been called into the headmaster's office. She prepared to feel ashamed about why she was there.

'Hi, I'm Jessica White and I'm the managing director of Smiths' Solicitors. You're here for a divorce, is that correct?' She barely even looked at Rose as she offered her a seat, but down at the form she'd filled in.

Rose sat down and took a deep breath thinking it was a lot to explain but she started with the email and showed it to Jessica.

Jessica White shook her head. 'OK, so the divorce is going to have to wait because you're in court on Monday and it's Friday today. We're going to have to get a witness statement together now and I'll have to get hold of a solicitor in York to attend with you. It's going to be £500 before VAT and I would suggest you don't go unrepresented to this court case.'

'Shit,' Rose replied as Jessica raised her eyebrows over her glasses. 'Erm, sorry… OK, we'll do that. How do I pay?'

Jessica explained that a card payment would need to be made before 4.00 p.m. today and she'd find a solicitor in York and pass them all the information and it would be handled as a priority.

Rose knew she had to say yes and then sort it out by phoning everyone to beg for more help. This was a matter of keeping the children with her or losing them to Darren. The battle was just about to start, and Rose didn't feel at all prepared, where was she going to get £500 from?

Jessica continued, 'OK, so let's sort this meeting out first; I'm going to need to know everything, every reason why the children should stay with you and not him.'

Rose pulled out the folder full of evidence against Darren which she'd prepared. She thought that the most important thing would be the discharge letter from Harrison's recent stay, but she was also armed with photographs she'd taken of the children over the last few weeks, showing them in dirty clothes, unbathed, messy haired, and generally unkept. She even had a mouldy dummy that Harrison had been using when she collected him one day. Grateful for her foresight at recording things Darren said, she had those on file too, along with screen shots of his vile emails and text messages, and details of every call she'd had to make to the police and social services.

Pushing it towards Jessica, she said 'I've been on my own for a few weeks now and it's all I've thought about. Tim and I started to collate everything we thought might help. Darren has stolen and ruined the last six years of my life, I won't let him do the same to my children.'

Half an hour went by and so her free time was gone, Jessica could see Rose looking at her watch repeatedly and reassured her that the price was capped and so it won't go over the quote price, Rose was still wondering how this money was going to get to the solicitors. The main factors of the situation were discussed, Jessica questioned Rose like she was in an interrogation, challenging different aspects of what Rose said about the relationship: why did it take her so long to leave him? Why weren't the police involved sooner? Why did he throw her out? It felt as if she was repeating herself like she was back in the police station with PC Samson.

When it was over, Rose explained to the secretary that she'd be back before 4.00 p.m. to pay the balance and she surprised herself at how convincing she sounded. Rose didn't know how on earth she was going to get this money together, but there had to be a way. Sell her phone? Sell what else, she didn't have much to her name.

Rose waited outside the solicitor's office in the mild air waiting for Tim to collect her, she'd explained everything on the phone when she called to tell it was over. She was hunched over, looking down at the ground, and feeling in need of a hug or a stiff drink, she couldn't decide. A few tears dropped to the ground, crying was the only thing Rose felt she was good at, at this current time. Rose was yet again in a daze when Tim pulled up in the lay-by nearest to her. He stepped out and helped her into the car as if she was unable to walk feeling weak at the knees. She gave him a slight smile and sat in the passenger seat of the car feeling sorry for herself.

Tim stroked her face and gave her a kiss on the cheek and said, 'You stay here with the kids and I'll go and have a word with the receptionist, OK?' Rose just nodded, not thinking to question him. She was mentally in a bad place and was wondering if she'd be out from under Darren's control. Should she go back? he'd warned her about this.

She couldn't lose her children. She'd been a full-time mother since the day Millie-Rose was born and she didn't know what she'd do without them.

'All sorted, nothing for you to worry about,' Tim said as he got back in to the car.

Rose was drained and just replied, 'Let's get home before Harrison gets upset with his chest.'

Tim drove them home wishing he could take all her worries away. He now realised that the hardest part wasn't bringing the kids here, it was going to be fighting Darren in court to keep them.

That afternoon, once Rose had dealt with the paperwork from the solicitor and organised for Lucy to babysit while she went to court on Monday, they spent hours playing hide-and-seek, making dens, and colouring with the kids. It was lovely to be 'normal' for a little while and put everything to the back of their minds.

It turned out to be a lovely afternoon, Tim had organised Lucy to babysit so that he and Rose could spend some time together. They had been cooped up in the hospital for the last few days and the days before that had been spent worrying about the move.

Tim noticed Rose wasn't really with him through the meal and he tried to talk about other things and 'get to know' Rose a bit more, like a proper date. Tim was understanding and supportive and the more they spent time together, the more Rose opened up to him and let herself trust him. It was going to take a long time to feel normal and the damage Darren had caused would never truly heal, but day by day, and step by step, Tim had promised to be there for her and the kids.

In bed that night, Rose couldn't stop the memories whizzing around her head, specifically, those just before she was thrown out into the street.

CHAPTER FOURTEEN

The weekend dragged out for Rose and Tim. The court case looming on the horizon was distracting them both and, although they were taking the children out and about, they couldn't help but think about what was going to happen on Monday.

The Designer Outlet near Liverpool had a large outdoor play area for children and Harrison and Millie-Rose were loving it. Tim and Rose were stood watching them when Tim said, 'They're great kids, you know?'

'Thank you,' Rose said quietly.

'I'm not just saying it, you've done a fantastic job with them.' Tim wanted her to see that someone recognised her abilities as a mother.

'If I was a good mum and if I'd done a good job, I would have left him sooner and not put them through all this.'

Rose was so disappointed with herself. 'I don't understand why you're even with me and doing this. Surely, you wouldn't want to be with someone like me, a failure, a disappointment. I mean... what do your parents think about all this? I know what I'd be thinking if it was one of my children and they were giving up everything to help someone with two children and going through all this crap.'

'My parents support me and the decisions I make, no matter what they are–'

'That doesn't mean that they agree or like your decision, though.' Rose interrupted.

'You can't fight me on everything, Rose, why are you even worried about my parents, anyway?'

'Because, Tim, you mean something to me and I care about what they think… I want them to like me.'

Tim let out a light sigh, 'Let them help and as they do, they will get to know you and they'll not just like you, but they'll love you too, because you're caring, creative, funny, loving, and of course you have a good head on your shoulders.'

Rose elbowed him bashfully and shrugged off the compliment. 'You're just saying that.'

'You may not think so but that's still my opinion! You're always reluctant to accept anything nice I say about you and I want to change that; I want you to see yourself the way I do.'

Rose gave Tim a peck on the cheek and they continued to watch Millie-Rose and Harrison who were starting to compete with each other on who could climb the highest on the frame. 'I never said thank you, did I?' Rose suddenly remembered that if it wasn't for Tim she wouldn't have a solicitor on Monday.

'What for?' Tim asked.

'For the solicitor, I will pay you back you know…' and Tim interrupted Rose 'you already have, you have made a difference to me.' Rose could only think of all the bad differences she has likely made to Tim, 'I will pay you back because it's the right thing to do, it's not your baggage/

debt/problem to solve.' Tim just nodded knowing he'd never accept it or if he had no choice he'd simply give it back in a different way.

After a fun half an hour, they set off around the shops. Rose loved to window shop. Tim had told Rose that he was going to treat her as she, and the kids, needed some new clothes since they'd left with any of their belongings. Yes, we have a few things from your family, but I have some money to spend so let me spend it today.

Tim guided them to Next which thankfully wasn't that busy for a Saturday. The clearance sale racks were prominently placed, and Rose went hunting through the selection for the children; there were some nice clothes, but she'd never pay these prices for them, even if they were reduced.

'They've got plenty for the kids, haven't they?' Tim smiled and gestured to the selection.

'Yes, they do, but I'd never pay these prices, Tim.' Rose was trying to usher everyone back out the door. Tim insisted they stay and told the kids to have a look at whatever clothes they wanted. 'Now, you go and pick whatever you want,' he said to Rose.

Rose walked over to the women's clothes rack and looked through the selection, muttering to herself, 'Too small... too low cut... too slim fit... too big... too fancy... too expensive...' There was nothing that took her fancy, but she made an effort to carry on looking. Rose wasn't used to shopping for herself, she hadn't done it for years and rarely spent money on herself, it all went on her children and what they needed and wanted. She'd never forget the last time she was shopping with a man.

* * *

Rose thought it was quite amusing that now Darren, and she were separated, she was the slimmest she'd ever been, catching herself in the mirror she could see her collar bone and her jaw line was more defined. Rose's clothes were looking a little loose on her and she'd gone down a notch on her belt, she hadn't even looked closely at herself in the mirror until now. She looked poorly and as if she needed a good meal and some vitamins.

Rose was pulled out of her memories when Tim came over with Millie-Rose who was carrying a pile of clothes that she could barely see over the top. 'Look, Mummy, look, Mummy!'

She was so excited to show Rose what she'd chosen. Harrison wriggling around in Tim's arms to try to show Rose the shopping basket full of clothes for him.

'We needed another shopping basket,' Tim giggled. 'They loved choosing their own clothes.'

Tim and the children were laughing until Tim noticed that Rose had nothing in her arms.

'I can't find anything,' she said before he could say anything, 'and... I thought we could look another day, I'm tired and not feeling too well, anyway.'

They carried on shopping and Tim bought the children some toys and games. Rose thought Tim was showing too much confidence about the outcome of the court hearing, but she didn't say anything. The children were having too much fun. She hadn't seen them like this for a very long time.

They headed into Starbucks – it was like a glamorous afternoon out compared to the years of being hard-up for money with Darren. Rose didn't want to go in if she was honest, she'd promised not to step foot into a Starbucks again after the experience she had with Darren, she couldn't think about anything else but that memory. Memories like that just tainted any future moments. Today Rose couldn't stop the constant flashbacks.

Tim managed to make this experience a nicer one although he had no idea about what had happened in the past. Watching Tim and the children make milk moustaches and putting cream on each other's noses they had more fun than they'd had for years.

Rose wondered what life would have been like if she'd met Tim before Darren and skipped him altogether but, she couldn't forget that she wouldn't have her children if that had happened. Every cloud had a silver lining she supposed.

* * *

Millie-Rose and Harrison fell asleep in the car on the way home, so Tim and Rose scooped them out of their car seats and managed to tuck them into bed without waking them.

Once the kids were settled in bed, Tim started to organise the shopping which Rose thought was rather peculiar – Darren never did anything like that. She offered to help but Tim turned around to face her, smiled, and said, 'I was looking for this.' He handed her a Pandora gift bag.

'Don't think about it, don't fight it… just open it.'

Rose wasn't going to refuse but still felt like she couldn't accept it; she wasn't used to getting gifts and certainly didn't think she didn't deserve it. Carefully, she pulled the salmon pink ribbon and opened the bag to see a gift box, delicately, she opened the lid and the biggest smile she had in years. Gleaming up at her was a purple leather bracelet with a single charm hanging from it. An accent golden heart surrounded with tiny silver hearts.

Tim then explained, 'I chose this bracelet because this is

the start of your new life and I'm going to buy you a new charm for each step you take and achievement you make now that you're free. The first charm is there to remind you of the love you have shined out to me, the love you have for your children. You're the only woman I will love and I'm going to be with you every step in your new life.'

Rose was overwhelmed with love for Tim; tears filled her eyes, and she felt her knees go weak as he held her face and leant in to kiss her. Rose soon fell into Tim's kiss and shivers ran down her spine. Soon they were kissing hard and attempting to work their way through the living room and through the kitchen to get upstairs.

Lost in the moment, a trail of clothes had begun to follow them as Tim pulled her closer into his arms. He spun her around and pushed her against the fridge which rocked against the wall; he put his arms either side of her and kissed her, but Rose felt the urge to break free... she felt trapped and suddenly the memories of Darren holding her up against the fridge-freezer came rushing back to her. Rose went into a trance, she replayed it in her head and felt frozen in her body.

* * *

'Rose, Rose!' Tim was trying not shout, but he was panicking now. Rose was shaking, her breath was ragged, and tears were streaming down her face. *What the hell had Darren done to her?* he thought.

'I'm so sorry,' Rose started to apologise, 'I... I... I feel so stupid.'

'Stop it and don't tell me anything unless you want to.'

'You must think... you must think... I'm a nut case,' Rose was sobbing at the memory and the worry that this would be the melt-down that would make Tim run for the hills.

'You know whatever it is, I'm here, and I don't think you're a nut case, I just want to help you, we don't have to do anything until you're ready.'

Rose sobbed more. 'I wanted to, I was enjoying every minute of it... it was just... just... that you did something...'

'What did I do? Because I won't ever do it again. The last thing I want to do is hurt or upset you.'

Rose grabbed Tim's neck and pulled him in for a hug. 'I don't want to spoil anything; I'm falling for you.'

Tim smiled and said, 'You never have to worry about spoiling us – I'm in love with you and we can get through anything. I believe in us.' Rose pined for Tim and he said, 'Don't you remember? I was there right from the minute we met.'

Rose did remember, and she remembered how Tim changed her way of thinking from the moment he stepped into her life; he helped her gain a different focus which started with her business and giving her the confidence to strive to be successful. 'You will never know... you will never know exactly what you saved me from.'

'I don't need to know, and all you need to know now is that you're safe with me and I will look after you.'

That's all Rose ever wanted from a family: a husband to protect and look after her but Darren had ruined her ideas of what a marriage should be – Tim was trying to pick up the pieces and make the dream a reality.

CHAPTER FIFTEEN

Monday morning finally arrived, and Tim and Rose were on edge. Rose spent the morning chatting with some friends and business contacts online, but she couldn't concentrate, the court case was playing on her mind.

Deciding to try to relax, she laid on the bed and put the radio on. *'Would it make you feel better to watch me while I bleed?'*

Rose's ears pricked up, and she soaked up the lyrics that were being sung; she couldn't believe how she could relate to this song.

'You can take everything I have… go on and try to tear me down.'

Rose's heart was racing, and a wash of anger, upset, hatred, shame, and embarrassment came over her. *How did he get away with this? Why was I so naïve?* she thought.

Rose checked for the song on Shazam and found it was Ellie Goulding's *Skyscraper* and downloaded it onto her iPhone. She listened to it a few more times, it seemed to get her blood pumped and give her a new determination to fight for what was right and not let Darren treat her like a piece of shit on his shoe.

It gave her this instant courage and a sense of 'I can do this'.

Rose knew that this song was going to inspire her to keep going in the tough times to come and she knew she couldn't forget what Darren had done to her; this would remind her what he'd put her through if she ever felt that she should stay with him, if her nerves ever wavered, if her confidence ever slumped, this song would the one that would make her think and remember that feeling coming from the pit of her stomach.

The journey to the court seemed to take hours, but it passed in a blur. Rose had asked a couple of her family and friends to be there, knowing that Darren would turn up mob-handed with his family. She thought she'd be able prepared and show them she's not on her own.

Having never been in court before, Rose was anxious at the nerved she felt just by walking through the metal detectors. She instantly felt like a criminal when the alarm went off and she had to have the wand scanned over her by the security guard. Once through, she couldn't see Darren or his family anywhere but met with her barrister.

He summoned Tim and her into a side room to discuss the case. He had clearly done his homework and was earning his fees. He was a well-kept man who reminded her a little of an older Harry Potter with his round spectacles and the way he styled his dyed hair.

Once they'd run through everything, he went to find out if Darren had arrived and to check some other barrister-type things and shuffling the paperwork.

The barrister found Darren sitting in the waiting room, he was representing himself, so he gave him a copy of the statement Rose had put together over the weekend to fight her case.

As Darren read the statement, he didn't realise that the

couple sat opposite him were Tim's parents. They watched him as muttered swear words to himself – he clearly hadn't thought she'd fight back, and certainly not by telling the court everything.

Back in the side room, Rose was starting to panic, she knew that the information she'd provided was going to have repercussions, but she just hoped that it wouldn't affect her children too much.

Eventually, they were called in to court and Rose sat with the barrister in between her and Darren. It wasn't until the judge walked in that she realised she had no idea what the barrister's name was.

Looking at the judge, she realised that she'd lost all her control. Just when she thought she'd escaped being controlled by Darren, one of the most important decisions that would ever be made about her life, was now out of her hands. Completely. Her children. Their future. Was in the hands of the intimidating and authoritative man sat in front of them. Looking up at the ceiling Rose had never prayed so hard in her life.

They started with her barrister giving the case summary due to Darren being unrepresented. The judge wanted to hear from Darren first because he was the applicant and so he was to give his reasons for his application to court first.

'She took the kids from me last week and I have no idea where or how they are.' Darren replied.

The judge started questioning the barrister; if this was the case why Darren didn't have an address.

Rose had to whisper points to the barrister because how would he know every little detail or reason? The police had advised her not to give an address out due to risk of harm on her and the children.

Rose could see Darren smirking from the corner of her

eye and was devastated at the judge's first decision, that he was entitled to know where his children were living, even though the police had told her to keep it from him.

* * *

The judge was distressing and wouldn't let Rose's barrister complete a sentence. He kept interrupting him and asking Darren what his point of view was. Darren was a master manipulator and within no time at the all, the judge was on his side. He was disregarding everything in Rose's statement and allowing Darren to twist it around so that it appeared to be all her fault.

Rose felt it was like being back in each situation once again, she thought to herself *I had dug so deep within myself to do this, to leave him, to get my children, to tell people what had happened to me, what I had endured, paid the price and now this. Why had I even bothered?*

Rose was bewildered by the discussion and she'd turned off from reality until it finally reached the point when Harrison had been admitted to hospital and the piece of evidence from the doctor accounting his admission to hospital to be a direct result from neglect.

The judge's face changed and now he had a scorn on his face, he looked foolish, it was surreal. He looked like a child who had just had his Christmas presents stolen.

'We need to pass this to the courts near where the children are currently residing, and I suggest that they stay with their mother for the time being until the next hearing where we will schedule a longer session to decide the outcome of residency.

'This will be held within the next three months. There is to be access one day a week and the parents are to discuss this outside of court with Barrister Redford.'

Then the judge stamped his paperwork, didn't even look towards Rose or Darren and dismissed them out of the courtroom. The position had completely changed for Rose, she made her way back to the side room with the barrister and Darren was directed to a side room on his own.

'I'm going to go and find out what Darren will want, there's no point us making an offer to the judge first as I doubt he'll accept it. It will save us time to do it this way, I think,' Mr Redford said.

The wait for the barrister to come was a long one. Tim was going through various options, talking through what had been in said and as he carried on, Rose's head was spinning. She didn't what she'd expected, but it wasn't that. She stood up and told Tim she was going to get some water, the last thing she remembered was the ground rushing towards her as if it had developed hands and they were reaching out to take hold of Rose.

* * *

Rose was soon woken by a splash of water on her face with Tim and his parents looking down over her; she came round fast and Tim helped her up and gave her a kiss on the cheek. 'It's the stress, Rose, come on, it won't be long now, you don't want Darren knowing about this and thinking he's won; you're stronger than that.'

Tim picked her up and helped her back to her seat. Thankfully, the barrister wasn't back yet. Tim's mum had a stash of snacks in her handbag and handed Rose a chocolate bar. 'You haven't eaten this morning love, eat this – the sugar will do you good.'

Rose accepted it to be polite – she'd only known Tim's

parents a few weeks – and she forced half a bar down within a minute. It was very much welcomed.

Eventually, the barrister dawdled back in to the room and sat down next to Rose. 'OK,' he said, 'Darren would like access to be on a Friday from 11 to 5. He'd like you to drop them off to his home in York and he will return them to your home in Liverpool.'

Tim saw Rose starting to panic and so he spoke for her, it was like he knew what was going through her mind, 'I don't think going to either home is an option considering the domestic violence mentioned; I think it would be best to meet in a public place instead and I think Rose would feel more comfortable with this too.'

Rose nervously nodded and got out a few words, 'I'm... not feeling... too good... my head... is splitting. I don't care... about it... being on a Friday... and those times... let's give... him that... be amicable.'

The barrister agreed and, after he'd written down their response, he went to tell Darren their decision.

It took several messages back and forth for the barrister before it was all sorted out and they finally agreed that they would meet Darren at a supermarket within walking distance of Darren's house. He didn't drive so Rose had to make the concession to do the travelling. She didn't want to go too close to his house in case his family and friends started playing games.

Rose didn't want to have to go back into the courtroom and see the judge again. She'd seen him look down his nose at her like she was a second-class citizen. She'd wanted to scream that her children were her life, they were wanted, they weren't accidents that she was using as pawns in a game with her ex, but she couldn't say anything like that. Confrontation wasn't in her nature.

When their names were called to go back to the courtroom, Rose felt the bile rising in her throat and, with a swig of water, she held her head high, but her confident face mask on and followed the barrister through the doors. Rose remembered back to Christmas Day and the two hours of time she was allocated to see her Millie-Rose and Harrison.

* * *

Rose felt a rush of warm feelings thinking about how Tim was so supportive from such a horrible situation. It made her lift her chin and push her shoulders back; she walked into the courtroom as confident as she could knowing that no matter what happened, Tim would be waiting for her when she walked back out.

Rose wasn't gone long, and she even held the door open for Darren on the way out, her confidence beaming out of her. She was happy with the outcome and she wanted to feel in control for once. Rose told Tim and his parents that it had simply been a case of them signing the draft court order and having to adhere to it until the next court hearing. The judge let them leave with a few words of warning on both of their parts and Rose couldn't stand the fact that the judge was making assumptions.

'Don't use the children as weapons because it will come back to bite you both when they are older, and these children deserve to have the best upbringing they can.'

The barrister came to shake their hands and told them he would email the draft to her solicitors along with the proceedings and a load more legal jargon that Rose pretended to understand.

Tim walked out of the front door of the courts with Rose in his arms.

Tim got some tissues out of her handbag and said, 'It wasn't ever going to be easy, but we're one step closer, you should look at this like a victory, part of the battle is won.' There was a short silence. 'Rose, I'm so proud of you! For facing it and having to be open about what happened to you.'

Rose started giggling, 'I couldn't have done it without you, don't you see? You've been the one to show me how to stand up for myself and that I have no choice but to be true to my side because it depends on where the children will be. To not give up even when you down on the ground with nothing to look up to.' Tim embraced Rose, and she left a wet patch on his suit jacket.

Rose added, 'No one has ever told me they're proud of me and it means more than you could ever know to hear it from someone who truly believes in me and cares for me and loves me... I can't ever thank you enough.'

'Let's get back to my parents' house; they have champagne waiting. I suggest you ring your mum and dad too.' James and Sarah climbed into the car after paying the car parking charge and although they gave words of encouragement to Rose, she couldn't help being worried about what they thought of her and who she was currently married to. What they thought about their son's girlfriend. Trash? That's what she thought would be running through their minds.

After an almost silent journey back to their house, Tim's parents welcomed her in with hugs and happiness at the outcome of the hearing and Rose felt grateful that even though she had her doubts about their feelings towards her, at that moment in time, she couldn't have felt more at home. This fight was going to be hard, really difficult, but it was going to be worth it, and she could do it, she just needed someone to prop her up for a bit while she regained her strength.

CHAPTER SIXTEEN

Tim's parents had invited a couple of family members and close friends over to their house to welcome them home. Rose couldn't help wondering what would have happened if the decision had gone the other way? But she stopped those thoughts because she felt a sense of freedom from the suffocation she'd endured for the past six years. The divorce would come, yes, but this was a fight for a beginning and a long journey awaits the end.

Surrounded by Tim's family and friends, Rose felt a little strange, she knew that they were all happy for her and as the day carried on. The champagne was flowing, and laughter was all around her.

Rose grinned at Tim as he came up and offered her a top-up. 'Go on then,' she replied, 'I'm just going to nip to the loo. I won't be a minute.' Rose went upstairs and straight to the toilet where she was sick. She immediately felt better and put her head under the tap at the bathroom sink and washed out her mouth.

She knew the champagne would wash the taste out and she was determined that she wasn't going to let Darren ruin anything else in her life. Tim was waiting for her and as she walked downstairs, he handed her another glass of champagne and had a dish of salted peanuts. It reminded Rose of New Year's Eve with everyone holding glasses of champagne, eating nibbles, and in conversations.

Tim gave her a kiss on the cheek as she passed and placed his hand on her lower back to guide her into the celebrations. James and Sarah were looking over at them with smiles on their faces. Rose, finally feeling stronger and able to stand up straight, was wondering what she'd missed and went over to speak to them.

'Thank you so much, Sarah,' and Rose gave her a hug and a kiss on the cheek. 'Thank you, James, you don't know how much this all means to me.' And Rose gave Tim's dad a hug and a kiss on the cheek.

Sarah beamed at Rose and said, 'Look, this is what our family is about, and this is what we do; it was a pleasure to help and thank you for letting us.'

Rose interrupted, 'But you shouldn't have to, and you've done so much more than I'd ever expected. I guess I'm trying to say to you that you have only known me for such a short time, but you have put everything aside and treated me like you have known me for years.'

Sarah interrupted back. 'Now come on… you don't need to say it, let's enjoy celebrating and have a break from thinking about it all.'

Rose smiled. 'Yes, you're right.' Tim then clinked his glass to get everyone's attention.

'Can I have everyone's attention, please?' Rose had already started to blush. She hadn't got the chance to talk to James' and Sarah's family and friends yet.

'Hi, everyone. I know you're all busy and want to grab Rose for a chat… but I felt I had to just say a couple of words. First, thank you to my parents, whose footsteps I will continue to walk in as they are selfless and not at all frivolous. When I came to them and explained who I'd met and that I needed to help her with their support.'

Rose was bright red and filled with guilt and shame. 'When they met Rose, which wasn't that long ago, they could see what I see and that's a beautiful young woman who loves to work hard and puts everyone else before herself.'

Rose's ears started to turn pink, and she was shaking her head. 'I would like us all to raise a glass to her because today she deserves to be celebrated as she put herself outside her comfort zone and I can't tell you just how courageous this lady is. Let's raise a glass to Rose.'

Rose was trembling as everyone held up their champagne flutes towards her and said, 'To Rose!' in unison. Rose then returned a slightly raised flute with a thank you grin and went to take a sip when something hard touched her lips that wasn't the glass or the champagne. Confused and curious, and she looked into her glass and inside she could see a glint and a sparkle within the bubbles of the champagne.

Tim had arrived in front of her and gave her a look as if to say, *everything will be OK*. He slowly got down onto one knee. Rose was as speechless as the rest of the room.

Tim held her hand and looked up at her. 'Rose, I don't know the half of what you have been through, but I know that you're an incredibly brave woman; you never deserved to have been treated that way. I want to help you forget the pain and find happiness. I want to be the person that helps you stand up when you feel that you can't. I want to be the person you can confide in and trust unlike what you have had before. I'm bewildered by you as a person; you're not only intelligent, creative, and hard-working but you're the most beautiful woman I've ever met.'

Rose was welling up and shaking her head. She didn't believe what Tim was saying. 'You may shake your head, but I want to help change that. I want to help you see all the things I see in you and build your self-confidence up because you should be proud of yourself and the person you are.

'I must now say that above all of this you're a mum and your two children are so lucky to have you; they are such wonderful children and you have protected them since they were born and now they are a credit to you. If you will let me, I want to be a part of your family and I want to help you protect them in the days, weeks, months, and years to come. I see your love for them and it's infectious.'

Rose had tears rolling down her face and Tim hadn't taken his eyes off her; everyone in the room was transfixed on them both and could see the connection between them.

'So, if I may take your hand.' Rose blushed, wiped her tears with one hand and gave her other hand to Tim, who took the ring from Rose and got ready to slip it onto her finger. 'Rose Stephanie Shaw... will you let me join you on your journey and let me show everyone my commitment to Millie-Rose, Harrison and you?...Will you marry me?'

Rose looked around at all of Tim's family expecting someone to stop him from making a stupid mistake but they all smiled at her. Sarah and James had come to a place they could see, James's had his arm around Sarah and they were embraced, sharing a smile and were ready to toast with their champagne.

Rose couldn't believe how secure she felt with Tim and his parents. Everyone was waiting for her answer and Rose took a deep breath – she knew what she wanted to say and didn't want to hesitate any longer but what if she was jumping into another situation like what she'd just escaped?

She told herself she'd give it time with Tim, it was vital

she and her children were safe. She saw Tim looking up at her like a lost puppy waiting for her response. Rose had a sudden moment of realisation. *I was branded, branded like I was his possession, his object, his everything,* she thought to herself and felt the top of her shoulder; she could feel the scar and held back her breath. *Tim hasn't told me I'm his, he has said I can do what I like, and he wants to support me and the children,* a tear crept out of her eye and slid down her cheek and then she felt a warm rub on her hand and looked down.

It was Tim stroking her hand. Rose could feel the warmth from his hand flow up her arm. She'd never felt like this – felt like someone cared for her, loved her, and would give up everything for her. Tim was affectionate, and it was one of the things missing from her life. Rose began to feel happy, and she hadn't felt anything like it before; she'd forgotten what it was like to feel a sense of happiness.

Slowly, she knelt and joined Tim on the floor and held his hand back. 'I will marry you but not only that, I want to promise you that I will try, I will try to find refuge within myself so that you aren't shadowed by my past. It won't be easy, and I ask that you're patient with me. I know I need to believe in myself and believe in you, I have no reason to doubt you and I will try my best not to.'

Rose helped Tim put on the ring, a simple and elegant tiffany cut diamond with a platinum band. Tim had tears in his eyes and Rose had them rolling down her face, both with the widest smiles in the room. They both giggled, and that was everyone's cue to applaud and cheer. Tim leant towards Rose, still kneeling on the floor and kissed her lips tenderly. They got up from the ground still embracing with a kiss which slowly turned into a hug. Rose felt the warm embrace of his security and let him hold her. Tim's family came huddling around them and cuddling them like one big pile-on; they all believed in them as a couple and were there to support them.

Tim and Rose shared a glass of champagne and Rose thought it was best to mention something she thought Tim hadn't considered. 'You have to ask the children for their approval yet, you know?' Tim's face went from wide-smile to concerned and they both laughed together.

Rose said, 'Don't worry, they already love you and I think they would love to have you as their stepdad.'

Rose giggled again thinking Tim wouldn't have thought about being a dad, but he smiled back and said, 'Rose, I can't wait to start,' and he kissed her on the lips. 'Now, let's get everyone drunk in celebrating with us; you haven't seen my mum when she's had a few – it's a good job there's no karaoke.'

Rose giggled again, looking over at his mum who was already hiccupping and on her fifth glass of champagne. She looked around and could see smiles and celebration all around her; family and friends who were supportive and caring. It was all she'd ever wanted. Tim was all she'd ever wanted. Among this mess, she'd found the love of her life and she hoped that everything would work out fine.

Wouldn't it?

.

ABOUT THE AUTHOR

Born in the North East, Jennifer is a young, married mum with three children. In addition to being an author, she is an entrepreneur, running a family business from her home-base. Her blog posts have a large readership of other young mums in business.

From an early age, Jennifer has had a passion for writing and started gathering ideas and plot lines from her teenage years. A passionate advocate for women in abusive relationships, she has drawn on her personal experiences to write this first novel.

It details the journey of a young woman from the despair of an emotionally abusive and unhappy marriage to develop the confidence to challenge and change her life and to love again.

A note from the Author

I hope that in reading my book, I will raise awareness of this often hidden and unseen behaviour and empower women in abusive relationships to seek help for themselves and find the confidence to change their lives.

If you have been affected by what you have read in this book, you are not alone, talk to someone and take the first step out of isolation. Or you can call the 24 hour free-phone National Domestic Violence helpline on 0808 2000 247.

There are national and local charity and council-led helplines, so I urge you to make that call, if it's safe.
If you are not in the UK I am sure there are support lines of a similar nature.

Jennifer

www.jennifergilmour.com
www.facebook.com/isolationjunctionbook
www.instagram.com/authorjennifergilmour
www.twitter.com/jenlgilmour